A chemical engineer from IIT Roorkee, **Shilpa Gupta** holds a post-graduate degree in management from IIM Ahmedabad. After working as an investment banker for thirteen years in Mumbai, she relocated to Pune in 2007 and quit her corporate career a couple of years later to take care of her two growing boys, Aditya and Ritwik. Apart from mathematics and finance, her interests lie in meditation, writing, painting and travel. Shilpa is married to Sriram, her batchmate from IIT Roorkee. While she has many published financial research papers to her credit, *Ananya* marks her debut into the world of fiction.

a bittersweet journey

Ananya

SHILPA GUPTA

RUPA

Published by
Rupa Publications India Pvt. Ltd 2015
7/16, Ansari Road, Daryaganj
New Delhi 110002

Sales centres:
Allahabad Bengaluru Chennai
Hyderabad Jaipur Kathmandu
Kolkata Mumbai

ISBN: 978-81-291-3514-8

First impression 2015

10 9 8 7 6 5 4 3 2 1

The moral right of the author has been asserted.

Typeset at SÜRYA, New Delhi

Printed by Parksons Graphics Pvt.Ltd, Mumbai

To the people from whom I have learnt the most and with whom
I continue falling a little bit more in love every day.
You complete me.

Mom,
Sriram,
Aditya and Ritwik,

and Dad, my role model. I miss you.

Prologue

When I opened my eyes, I was on a stretcher being wheeled inside a hospital. I saw a white-faced, frantic-looking Ma walking beside me. Tubes were glued to my arms and I faintly heard Ma say, 'Anu, what happened? Tell us.' I opened my mouth but no words came out. I looked away from her. 'Don't worry, Beta, you will soon be fine; God is with us!' As I weakly opened my eyes to look at her, I felt very drowsy and soon I felt myself slip into blissful oblivion yet again.

'Did she say anything? Who was it?' The thing I'd dreaded the most, happened in the evening—Pa came to visit me. He asked Ma this question hesitatingly. The fall from grace of his darling daughter—the one he doted on and who he always took pride in showing off to the world—was so steep that probably he couldn't orient himself. 'You know Sudha, I can't believe what has happened. Our Ananya? She always stood taller than others; she was the class prefect, a topper! Where did we go wrong?'

I kept my eyes shut; it was easier to continue pretending to be asleep. However, I felt a touch on my hand and slowly opened my eyes. Papa had come to sit next to my bed—my father, who had so much faith in me, loved me unconditionally.

His head was bent. He looked tired and beaten. His face was unshaven and his white shirt crumpled. A tear rolled past my closed eyes. 'Papa,' I said softly. As he looked up, I was shocked; it seemed as if the light had gone from his eyes.

Papa wiped my tears with his hand and then he stood up and left the room without saying a word. That hurt me more than any remonstration would have.

Book #1

Incy wincy spider climbed up the water spout

1

Till Class X, I was in the same section as my closest friends and we had a whale of a time. However, in Class XI we selected different streams. Nandini had taken arts, Sanjana commerce, and Moh had opted for science with biology, while I had taken up science with computers. We met during lunch breaks or for a few common classes like English and math, which took place on Fridays. This is the reason I looked forward to Fridays the most.

Each of us excelled at something; I really doubt that I would have made friends with 'ordinary girls' who were just average. It was nothing conscious or deliberate, probably just the way I was. I guess the fact that we all followed different streams, besides intellectually enriching our group was also the reason for the longevity of our friendship. There was no hierarchy in our group, no petty jealousies and we never competed directly in any area. Since we all had our own lives to lead and our own passions to follow, ours was not a parasitic relationship either.

While I looked forward to the opportunity of being with my friends during this time, the English teacher, Ms Simran, was one of my least favourites. I had never once seen her repeat her sarees in the entire semester and today was no exception. She was wearing a beautiful, light yellow cotton saree. While the saree was compulsory for all women teachers, she was the only one who managed to make a fashion statement out of it. Her sleeveless blouses, high heels and long nails— always polished bright red—lent her glamour that was missing in the rest of the teachers. Boys never missed her class. However, she had a peculiarly grainy, nasal voice that grated on my nerves.

As I looked across the classroom, I saw Moh's bench partner Kabir suppress a yawn while she herself looked interested and was listening to the lecture with rapt attention. Dev was playing book cricket with Dhruv. Dev was probably the handsomest boy in the entire class, or at least Sanjana thought so. Sanjana, though in a different section, had a thing for him and often sighed when he didn't show any interest in her. She would constantly pester Moh and me for details about him and became exasperated with our lack of interest in the 'hunk'. Nandini's passion was sketching, which she pursued almost anywhere and everywhere. Out of curiosity, I leaned over to see what she was drawing and was shocked to see a perfect caricature of our teacher! Nandini was talented, no doubt, but was taking a humungous risk this time. I shuddered to think what would follow if she got caught, although I envied her skill and indifference.

I looked at my bench partner and long-time family friend, Amit. We had been sharing the desk in the last row for as long as I could remember. Both of us were the tallest in our respective genders and the desks were allocated on the basis of height. I was not surprised to see him industriously taking notes. While I had been daydreaming, he had filled pages with his spider-like handwriting. This finally spurred me into action. It didn't matter if I liked English or not, it was a scoring subject and I was not willing to cede even a tiny bit of ground to Amit. A dear friend though he was, he was also my arch rival. I forced myself to focus and furiously started taking down notes.

Suddenly, something dropped on my desk. It was a lizard and its tail was moving. I screamed mindlessly since I was petrified of lizards. To my horror, I heard a few boys sniggering. Ms Simran, also known to be the strictest teacher in school, walked up to me and asked, 'What's the matter Ananya?' in a tone that could have frozen any mortal. I was too scared to even open my mouth.

I pointed at my desk and to my surprise, the lizard had disappeared. I tried telling her this, but she didn't believe me. In her screechy voice, she said, 'Ananya, in spite of being the prefect, you are disturbing the whole class. Please leave right now and go to the detention room.' Shamefacedly I muttered, 'Sorry ma'am,' and started going when Amit got up and said, 'Ma'am, please don't punish her. It was my fault. She screamed because I threw a plastic lizard at her.' He produced the slimy-looking thing from his pocket that had a thread attached to its tail. I gagged.

Ms Simran, who had been irritated with me, was now furious. 'Both of you leave the class and take that wily thing with you,' she said. She also shuddered at the sight of that lizard—so I wasn't the only one! I was however enraged with Amit, who followed me into the detention room. But I eased as I thought that at least he had owned up. At the same time, it was too mean a trick. I decided that I was never going to forgive him.

In the detention room I went and sulked in a corner ignoring Amit. But he still had the nerve to come and sit next to me. He immediately began apologizing, saying he did that only to get a rise out of me. He said he hadn't meant any harm and since I had been looking very bored for most of the class, he wanted to see a different expression on my face. As I looked at him with accusing eyes, he conceded that the joke had gone too far and he had never really thought it would result in us being thrown out of class.

He apologized again and he looked so comically contrite that I was compelled to forgive him. Really, it was impossible to stay cross with him for long. Seeing me melt, Amit was in his element again. He mimicked Ms Simran, and recalled how she had gone red in the face when she saw the lizard and how she had then ordered us both out, eyes blazing, cheeks puffed and her voice more nasal than ever. He had me in splits; he was a really good mimic.

2

Naphthalene balls. It was always the smell of naphthalene balls in our house that heralded the onset of winter. Mom would open the trunks, shake out the woollens and sun them for a day. The smell never really went away completely. Not that I minded, I quite liked the odour, just as I liked that of petrol, wet paint, nail polish remover and Fevicol. Maybe my brain was wired differently or maybe everyone liked these smells; I don't know. I would like to think the former, as I definitely didn't want to be a part of 'everybody'.

The memory of the humiliation in Ms Simran's class on that Friday had not faded properly when the next mishap happened a couple of Fridays later in that doleful winter. I have reasons to believe that Fridays were jinxed for me. Or at least that is what I believed then, though it was a Saturday that turned out to be the most jinxed day of my life. Next to math, physics was my favourite subject though its instructor, Shastriji, was completely loony. Always dressed in a stark white shirt and trousers that he paired with impeccably shiny black shoes, he was tall and had a long, sharp nose. His huge forehead always sported a chandan tilak. He kept his head shaved, except for a small spot at the back where he let his hair grow long. He came from a highly respected Brahmin family in Kashi and it was rumoured that he had lost an argument with our principal on whether he could teach in a dhoti-kurta. He was a perfectionist and we pitied any student who invited his wrath. When he got angry (which was often), his roar was the result of the lung power of 108 generations of his forefathers trained to incessantly chant mantras at the top of their voices. He had no sense of humour but his knowledge of the subject was incredibly good. This was reason enough for me to worship the ground he walked on whether I personally liked him or not.

Fortunately, I had always managed to escape his wrath and thanked my guardian angel at the end of each class. I was particularly excited that day, as we were to study electromagnetism, which I found extremely fascinating. But today, Shastriji asked us to shut our books and put them away. Most of the class groaned, as we all knew what this meant—a surprise quiz. His quizzes never had out-of-the-book questions, but involved a fair bit of lateral thinking which actually made them quite interesting. Unlike the others, I always looked forward to them.

As I finished my quiz and got up, I saw Moh returning to her seat. I smiled to myself. Moh was the only student in class who could solve problems faster than me. Amit just about matched me.

As I sat down, Amit dropped a ball of paper on my desk. The note was in Moh's writing. I smiled as I read:

Ananya, Sanjana, Nandini,
    Sleepover at my place tonight? Pass on the note and let me know.

Today was Friday and what better way to spend the evening! I wrote a 'Yes!' and folded the note.

I nudged Dev and hissed under my breath for him to pass it on to Nandini. This was when Shastriji swooped down on me and bellowed, 'What is in your hand?' I cringed, opened my palm and waited for the verdict. I stood up, cheeks burning and embarrassed to the core with thirty-six pairs of eyes burning me. Shastriji's face turned red as he read the note. He hollered, 'Ananya! of all students, this kind of indiscipline is unexpected from you! PASSING NOTES IN THE CLASS! Ananya, Sanjana, Nandini and Mohini, you all will miss your lunch break on Monday and go for detention where I will give you a test. And now, all you four young ladies may leave my class and stand outside!'

While I burned scarlet with shame, Moh was least affected. Nandini, as was her habit, chewed on her lower lip with nervousness and Sanjana stuck out her tongue as soon as Shastriji's back was turned. Shastriji just didn't understand us—we could have fun and also do well in our studies. He was a khadoos, I grumbled. Sulking even more I thought had we been allowed mobile phones in school we could have conducted this business with quiet dignity.

Luckily, the bell rang within minutes and we slunk back into the classroom to get our bags and run to catch our school buses. As I picked up my bag, some wayward words—spoken loud enough for me to hear—made their way to my ears, '...serves Ms four-eyed-goody-two-shoes right.' I didn't want to dignify this comment by giving 'Ms Aditi, the class duffer' a glance, and for good measure, pushed my specs firmly up my nose nonchalantly. I slung my bag on my back, squared my shoulders and walked off.

Despite my adopted nonchalance, her comment had rankled me. However, the prospect of going to Moh's house for a sleepover put me in high spirits. I shook my head trying to rid myself of the bad taste that Aditi's comment had left, telling myself that any comment from a person who had secured a position in the school's coveted science section not because of her marks—as was the case with everyone else— but because of her father being on the board of the school, was just not worth fretting over.

The sleepover at Moh's promised to be fun and these days I looked forward to these sleepovers even more, since we hardly met in school now. These sleepovers were amongst the very few distractions I allowed myself as I slogged my butt off trying to crack IIT-JEE.

3

'Are you a bi?' Sanjana asked me as I entered her room. Two sets of shoulders behind her shrugged helplessly as if trying to say, 'Don't ask us, we are not part of this!'

I tried to grapple with what Sanjana was saying. Bi—as in binary or bipolar? Then, when I saw the look of mischief on her face, the meaning of what she had asked slowly sank in and I shrieked, 'What?'

'Anu, don't act daft,' she said. 'You know what I mean. Are you bisexual—are you attracted to both guys and girls?'

'Sanjana, I know what bi means! And what kind of a question is this? For your kind information, at the moment I neither dig guys nor girls. Everything is on hold till I clear JEE, you know that. Now shut up!' Really! Sanjana could go a bit far at times.

'Oh come on Anu, don't be so stuffy. I didn't mean it in a real serious way, like a sexual relationship or something. But honestly, tell me, haven't you been attracted to any girl before? You know how many boyfriends I have had. But I'm attracted to girls as well! Yesterday, when I was having dinner with Luv, a particularly beautiful and curvy woman walked in; she looked so hot that I drooled at her along with my boyfriend!' Three pairs of eyes rolled as Sanjana finished, quite pleased with herself.

Sanjana had always had a shock quotient, which I suspect she cultivated deliberately and enjoyed secretly, but we were all very fond of her. However, for all her mischievousness, Sanjana was a very serious, truly talented classical dancer, totally passionate about her art form. But it had not always been so.

Her parents were accountants. They were good parents, warm and hard working, but knew or cared about very less beyond ledgers, audits and balancing books. Her mom didn't want Sanjana growing up as a uni-dimensional person like her. So, in an attempt to compensate for what she had missed in life, she put Sanjana in Kathak classes from the age of four. But to her mother's dismay, Sanjana did not show any interest in dance. In fact, the more her mother persuaded her, the more Sanjana rebelled. Sanjana would kick up a huge fuss or throw a tantrum before every dance class.

But her mother was equally determined. She would bundle up the kicking and screaming girl to her dance class thrice a week. This continued for as many as four years, a time that was hugely difficult for Sanjana.

But to everyone's surprise, including Sanjana's, she excelled at dance. According to her guruji, who was a direct descendant of one of the founders of the gharanas, she was a natural. As she grew older, her hatred for dance slowly diminished till, one day, she realized that she was cut out to be a dancer.

I had once accompanied her to one of her classes. She introduced me to guruji, her teacher. As the session began, I saw the infinite nimbleness in Sanjana's movements—she matched every challenge set by guruji. Teacher and disciple were both lost in high-pitch concentration, both unwilling to concede. There seemed to be a tangible stream of pulsating energy swirling around, binding the two of them. I was left awestruck.

I believe that even though Sanjana had finally found dance to be her true calling, having to cope with a dominating mother in her early years resulted in rebelliousness and an attention-seeking streak that could be seen in who she was now. Maybe this was just a part of her survival tactics for coping in an environment where no choices were allowed.

Now past the shock at Sanjana's scandalous question, I took a minute to look at my darling friends and smiled to myself.

The way we were dressed was a reflection of our personalities. Moh, the genius, was carelessly dressed as was her nature, down to her cargo pants and a baggy T-shirt teamed with an old pair of sneakers. She had a soothing personality, her pretty features always arranged in calm repose. Nandini was dressed in a light pink khadi-kurta over a white salwar. She would laughingly say that it was quite easy to caricature her own face, with its unusually high cheekbones. Sanjana was the prettiest of us. She had long thick hair, huge luminous green-blue eyes that twinkled above her full round mouth and under her black-winged eyebrows, each of which she could raise to make a point when needed. Today she was wearing a mauve halter-neck summer dress that showed off the dagger tattoo on her right shoulder; she had painted her nails in a colour matching her dress.

I looked at my reflection in the full-length mirror—at

5 feet 7 inches with stork-like legs, I was taller than most of my friends and as scrawny as a scarecrow. My friends had enviously tagged me as 'size zero', but it wasn't something I took particular pleasure in. They often wondered how, in spite of my appetite, I managed to stay stick-like. I don't know, maybe I had a high metabolism. My eyes though hidden behind my specs were probably my only attractive feature. They were like Mom's or so people said—big, almond-shaped and dark brown. Publicly I hated the comparison but secretly, I revelled in it. Often I had wished to be at least a fraction as beautiful as Mom, but would always shrug away the thought. What was not to be, would not be.

Rather than read mushy romances, which most of the girls my age were doing, I preferred spending my time with my math books or doing puzzles. I smiled at my reflection and tightened my ponytail. I turned back to my friends in time to hear Sanjana whispering mysteriously, 'Do you girls know what happened yesterday?' Since she could barely contain her excitement, I guessed it was something big.

We knew that madam had, of late, been favouring one of her admirers, a boy called Luv (and who actually had a twin brother called Kush. Eeks!) 'You know we went out last night for dinner. And at my door, after wishing me goodnight, he did something,' she said.

'WHAT?!' we echoed. 'He kissed me,' she stated with a flourish, raising her right black-winged eyebrow. This was BIG! We all stared at her with eyes round as saucers, falling out of their orbs. And then she blushed!

Voices trembling with excitement, we demanded, 'HOW was it?!' I mean, at 17, maybe it was not such an unusual thing to happen, but it surely was the first in our group.

She continued, 'Well, though I was very angry with him, honestly speaking, it was a rather nice feeling. Of course, it lasted only a few seconds, but now that I have been kissed once, I don't mind being kissed again.' She then sighed, looking at her painted nails, 'But I do wish he didn't have chapped lips.' *Chapped lips?* Was she crazy or what? In this larger picture, how did it even matter? She was our revered hero! We giggled in the night, whenever we imagined her kiss.

We pestered Sanjana to describe Luv. She said that they were connected on Facebook, so we quickly logged on. I don't know what I had expected, but Luv's photograph was like an anticlimax. He was too fair, had longish hair that curled around his collar and pink lips. He had a sort of vain look about him. To me, he looked quite effeminate. But perhaps it was a good idea to keep my thoughts to myself as I heard Nandini gasping and saw Sanjana blushing. Moh looked amused. Well, I was not into boys, but if I ever got interested in one, it would probably be someone diametrically opposite of Luv. Of course, he would need to be handsome, but not someone who was obsessed with his looks. And he would need to be tall so that I could wear heels and not feel conscious of him being shorter. But most importantly, he would need to be interesting, mature and intelligent, someone I could talk to, have discussions with and look up to.

Handsome but not vain. Tall. Interesting. Mature. Intelligent.

But the surprises were not over yet. Sanjana was not yet through with her shock quotient. She raised her T-shirt and to our saucer-wide eyes, a bellybutton ring, neatly pierced in her sunken navel, glistening against her ivory smooth skin, was revealed.

'Oh my God!' Moh recovered first, 'It is very beautiful.' 'Did it hurt?' asked Nandini in an awed whisper. 'Aunty allowed it?' was from a very impressed me.

'Thanks Moh. No, it didn't. And Aunty doesn't know about it,' replied the queen. 'But this one is not for Luv. I'm keeping it for Dev. Really, he is too good looking. But he does not even acknowledge my existence. I get so frustrated. But I'm not giving up on him. You all wait and see,' finished Sanjana dramatically.

'We are sure that you will have the poor guy in your net sooner or later,' I teased her half amused, half envious. I wished I had her carefree manner. Sanjana was always so high on life. Today, she had no worries, no super achiever parents, no serious goals to die for, no mood swings. Unlike me, the thought stuck me unbidden.

'I don't know when Dev will fall into my net. But you surely have Amit in yours,' said Sanjana to me. 'Oh, please! Don't pretend that you don't know about it. The poor guy's eyes are always tracking you. And you must admit he's not bad looking either.'

Amit? Amit was just a friend, a very old family friend, comfortable like an old, well-worn shoe. We shared a bench, exchanged notebooks, visited each other occasionally and most important of all, worked like maniacs to outdo each other in the exams. The curious case of the co-existence of our friendship and rivalry puzzled some and amused all. But Amit interested in me? Nah... too far-fetched. We were more like buddies. But I had to admit that in some teeny-weeny corner of my spleen, it pleased me to hear that a guy, *some* guy was interested in me. I had never thought that to be a possibility.

Anyway, I couldn't afford to waste time thinking about guys right now. Time for me was a precious commodity, a very precious one. I was just sternly reminding myself of this when the demented girl started chanting, 'Amit has the hots for Ananya! Amit has the hots for Ananya! And Ananya is blushing!' Oh so today, I was to be her target. But I wasn't going to let her get off easily. I grabbed a pillow and hit her. She grabbed another and retaliated. Soon, we looked like witches—our hair, clothes and goose feathers flying in every direction. I was giving her one more chase around the bed when the bedroom door flew open.

4

Handsome. Very much so.

Tall. I wouldn't need to worry about wearing heels with him.

Where did that stupid thought come from?

And Moh's brother, Rohit.

'Hi girls! What's up?'

'Seems that the whole gang is here. Let me see if I remember your names correctly—Nandini, Sanjana and you must be Ananya.'

Was it my imagination or did his eyes linger on me a fraction longer that they did on the others?

'Ananya, I almost didn't recognize you. God, you look different,' he added.

No, so it wasn't my imagination. He did look at me. And there was an expression in his eyes that I couldn't fathom. I felt butterflies fluttering in my stomach.

'Moh, can I have a minute with you? Goodnight girls,' he said as he closed the door softly after Moh followed him outside. However, I noticed her hesitation in doing so. I wondered why.

As Rohit left I suddenly felt like the side of a planet that had moved away from the sun—cold and dark. As I turned towards Sanjana and Nandini, I caught my reflection in the mirror. Oh no! In my pillow fight with Sanjana, my clothes had become disarrayed. My scrunchie had ridden down more than half the length of my ponytail and only a rat's tail remained tied in it. Most of my hair had come loose in untidy strands around my face. And there was a goose feather stuck in my hair and others on my clothes.

No wonder his eyes had lingered on me.

I looked like a complete clown. Looking at me, even Phool Kumari—the princess who never laughed—would not have had to wait for her prince to make her laugh. I would have sufficed. Maybe Phool Kumari was bi and would have gone for me.

What rubbish was I thinking? This was all Sanjana's doing.

And it dawned belatedly on me that the unfathomable emotion in his eyes had been a desperate attempt to control his laughter. At least, I had company. Sanjana must have looked the same. Thinking this, I cheered up and turned to look at her. She too looked dishevelled. But only slightly and very sexily so. I felt the twang of an unnamed emotion cut through me.

'Or maybe I will keep my bellybutton ring for Rohit. He's so very dishy,' Sanjana swooned.

In high spirits just sometime back, I now felt utterly miserable and very irritable.

'Sanjana, you really are the limit. You will go for anything that is male, especially someone who does not run in circles around you. At least show some decency sometimes,' I said.

Suddenly, there was complete silence in the room. Ear-splitting silence, louder than ten of my beloved Diwali atom bombs going off together. Sanjana stopped smiling, even Nandini dropped the book she was reading and started chewing her lower lip. I felt immensely uncomfortable and guilty.

'Anu, it is not like you to be so catty. I think you are upset with me because I teased you earlier about Amit. See, I'm sorry. I know these things don't interest you. And you are right, being Moh's brother, I guess Rohit is off limits. Say you are okay now?' Behind the jovial and extrovert girl was also a very sensible one. Seeing her look so contrite and being quite aware that I too had not been an epitome of politeness, I said, 'It's okay. I'm sorry too. Let's just forget the whole thing.'

Moh came back just then and looked a bit distracted. Since Sanjana and I were recovering from our argument, it was Nandini who did the needful.

'What's the matter, Mohini?' Nandini always called Moh by her full name.

'It's nothing.'

'Are you sure? You know you can share anything with us. You were quite fine till you went out with Rohit. Did he say anything?'

My ears picked up, but I didn't look at Moh.

'You are right Nandini. I have never kept anything from you guys. But well, this is a long story.'

'We love long stories,' Sanjana piped in and then added, 'Don't we, Ananya?' to further cement our camaraderie.

'Okay, listen then. You know Rohit went to the US for his Masters last year after finishing his engineering from IIT. He came home a couple of weeks back for his first term break.

Within days of his arrival, I discovered that he had taken to smoking. But he swore me to secrecy. You all know how close we both are. Against my better intentions, I agreed not to say anything but extracted the promise that he would quit at the earliest.'

'However, it was only a matter of time before my parents found out about it and they were terribly shocked.' I knew Moh's father well. Uncle was a highly respected professor and a Gandhian, highly principled. 'Mom talked to Rohit and he promised to give up smoking.'

'Then one day, Papa was working late in the night on one of his research papers. Past midnight, he went down to the kitchen and saw that the light in Rohit's room was on. Wanting to have a chat, he went over and knocked. There was no response and so he knocked again. Rohit opened the door after about 2–3 minutes. Though it was cold outside, all the windows of the room were open and a cold draught was blowing in. But even that could not take away the lingering smell of tobacco and alcohol. Papa just turned around and left.'

'I learned about the incident from Mom. I felt so disgusted. Today, in the evening when I discovered that he had gone out I went to his room. I found a pack of his cigarettes and a lighter in his cupboard drawer. I lit a cigarette and kept its burning end on one of his shirts, burning a hole in it. Then I gave the rest of his clothes—T-shirts, jeans, formal shirts, pants—the same treatment!'

On hearing this, and imagining a red-faced saint torching her brother's clothes, we couldn't stop laughing. Taking a breather from her laughter and wiping tears from her eyes,

Sanjana said, 'Imagine him dressed from head to toe with a hole in each of his garments.' Well, I didn't want to have any kind of picture of Rohit in my mind, but Nandini found it very amusing. Sanjana asked, 'What happened then?!'

Moh, slightly relaxed now, continued, 'Well, Rohit is stylish and has an extensive wardrobe. He just returned home from a party and found out about what I had done. He was appalled. Of course he figured out who the culprit was and that's why he came and called me.'

'Well, what did he say?' asked Nandini for whom the suspense was getting to be too much.

'I got the scolding of my life. I think he was itching to spank me; it was there in his eyes and if we both had been a bit younger, he may have done so. You all know what happens when water is added to sulphuric acid; it's a highly exothermic reaction. He kept hissing like that at me.' Moh loved these science-based metaphors. 'He's given me dire threats in case I dare go near his room ever.'

'What now? What happens to his smoking? What about your relationship with him?' it just slipped out from me.

'Oh don't worry. We will be fine; we have had worse fights and survived. He was already cooling down. And I think he will quit smoking. Plus as he sheepishly admitted, he will not be able to afford the habit now as he will need to save money out of his allowance to build up his wardrobe.'

Oh. Was it possible for any one day to be more eventful? A punishment by Shastriji and humiliation in the class, that duffer Aditi's comment, this sleepover at Moh's place, my petty argument with Sanjana and Moh burning up Rohit's wardrobe and getting into a fight with him—gosh, it really was too much!

However, the day had ended well. All was well in the world—Sanjana and I had made up. Rohit would quit smoking. Thankfully, I had put him out of my mind. Finally, we called it a day and went off to sleep in the early hours of the morning.

5

It was 9:30 am and still no sign of Papa's car. Despite sleeping late, we'd all woken up reasonably early, bathed, breakfasted and with the exception of me and of course Moh, everyone had left. I had to leave early too, but Papa had not turned up yet! Impatiently, I dialled his number.

'Pa, where are you? You were to pick me up from Moh's house, remember? I'm getting terribly late for my class.' I was punctual to a fault and I hated getting late for my IIT coaching classes. You didn't get into these revered institutes by being late for their entrance exam coaching classes.

'Sorry, Beta. I completely forgot. I know it's not excusable, but I got a call from the office. Some urgent work has come up and I'm on my way to office. Beta, can you please take an auto and go? I promise I will make it up to you later.' It was unlike Pa to forget but this meeting must be very important. But still I felt an acute sense of disappointment.

However, I knew that Papa loved me unconditionally and pampered me in whichever way he could. Despite a very hectic schedule, he always made time for me. He taught me swimming and badminton when I was a little girl and would often take me to his office on Saturdays for a while, where he would show me different machines and explain how they worked.

'Some urgent work has come up, Pa cannot make it,' I told Aunty. Out of my loyalty towards him, I could not add that he had forgotten. 'I will take an auto and go. I had a great time at your place. Bye Moh, bye Aunty!'

'Hey, where are you going? I can drop you,' Rohit said walking into the room, rolling up the sleeves of his dark blue shirt, which he had teamed with a pair of faded jeans.

'I'm just leaving for my coaching class. And I can manage; it's really not that far. I will take an auto and go.'

'What rubbish? Which ones do you go to? Deb's?' Upon my nod, he said, 'That's a sensible decision. They are the best ones in Pune. Grab your bag and I will drop you. Aren't you getting late?'

'Yes Beta, go with Rohit. We will also feel comfortable that you reached safely,' Aunty said.

Though the situation had gone out of my control, I didn't want to make a fuss about it. At least compared to last night, I now looked presentable in my white tee and jeans with my straight dark brown hair tied back neatly in a high pony with a multi-coloured scrunchie—the only concession I gave to colour. The no-fuss look of an IIT aspirant. 'Let me fasten the seatbelt for you,' Rohit said and before I could react he'd leaned over to pull the belt across me. As he did so his hand brushed lightly against the front of my tee. Though the touch was lighter than a paper fluttering under a fan, it created a riot of sensations in me. I felt confused, embarrassed, nervous and excited, all at the same time.

'Hey, I will come up too. As it happens, I went to these

coaching classes too. Let me just drop in and say hi to sir. It's been a long time since I met him,' he said.

For me, it was awkward being with Rohit and it would be more so in front of my classmates. But he left me with no option and came up with me. I saw the rest of the students waiting outside. There was the usual amount of din but the decibel levels came down when I walked in with Rohit. Everyone was trying hard not to look our way and I guess they were wondering what a plain Jane like me was doing with a hunk of a guy like Rohit. I felt very self-conscious and prayed for our class to start quickly. Suddenly, I felt as if someone was watching me. I looked around and suddenly made eye contact with Amit. I saw something akin to anger flash in his eyes a split second before he looked away. Instantly, I remembered what Sanjana had said last night about him and was flustered.

Just then we saw the students of the previous class pouring out. Good. Now we could go in and start the session with the paan-chewing Mr Gollum. His first batch of students had given him this name and it had stuck ever since. He had peppery, springy hair and a slight paunch which looked rather obscene on his wire-thin frame. He even muttered to himself while checking our papers.

Climbing the paan-stained staircase (which smelled of God knows what else) in a dingy building to reach an even dingier flat where our master ruled, I wished for the nth time that he would at least hold the classes in some decent place. I mean he made pots of money from these classes but was still so stingy. Gollum stepped out of the class to usher us in when Rohit stepped forward and said, 'Hello sir!'

'Rohit? I'm right no?' Gollum's face split into a wide smile, which revealed the full set of his paan-stained teeth. I almost fainted. The other students looked disgusted as well.

'How are you Rohit? MIT, huh? Not bad. One of my most favourite students.' He turned towards us and with a sweeping gesture, said in his usual vitriolic tone, 'Rohit was one of the brightest students in his class. And very hard working too. If you guys were half as smart and hard working, you would be through. But alas, this year, I'm stuck with this batch of underperformers.' Gollum had a split personality—a different code of conduct for his old, successful students and a totally different one for his current ones. Maybe if I also got through IIT, he'd bestow a smile on me too. Ugh!

However, I was super impressed with Gollum's praise of Rohit. It was unlike him. Rohit must really have been exceptional.

Handsome? Check. Tall? Check. Intelligent? Check.

We were quite used to Gollum's tirades and began filing into the room. I was just making my escape when I heard, 'Hey! Since your dad is busy today, let me pick you up after your class,' from Rohit. Before I could even say no, he had gone. My mind was in a haze throughout the class. I would need to copy the notes from someone later.

'You forgot the seatbelt again,' Rohit smiled at me and leaned across to fasten it, his hand brushing and lingering against the front of my tee a fraction of a second longer than last time. The earth completed a rotation on its axis in a split second. My head spun.

Late evening Moh called. Excitedly, she said, 'Rohit has bought three tickets for that movie you wanted to see and has asked me to invite you. You are on, right?' What made Moh, our saint-like friend, almost normal was her love of movies like the rest of us mortals.

I was torn between two feelings—at this moment, there was have nothing more I wanted than to go for a movie with Rohit. But I felt lost and confused about him as well. Did he invite me as Moh's friend to humour her or was he really interested in me? Also I wasn't sure about seeing him at all. Maybe if I avoided Moh for some time, I could also avoid him, as he would have left for the US by then.

'No,' I thought.

'Yes,' I said.

'Good girl,' said Moh.

I looked forward to the evening and got ready for the movie with nervous excitement. I put on a royal blue tee, the colour of copper sulphate, fastened my hair in a high ponytail with a bright red scrunchie and wore red shoes to match. My friends called my fashion sense eccentric, I called it non-existent. A huge collection of scrunchies in all hues and designs were my only fashion accessories.

Finally, evening arrived. Rohit and Moh drove up in their father's car. I was struck by Rohit's looks as I entered the car—he was wearing a white, short-sleeved shirt that was open at the neck and blue jeans. I was also impressed by the fact that he was driving the car himself; none of my friends were even eligible to touch a four-wheeler. Rohit looked so very grown up, smart and wise. In comparison, my classmates seemed like kindergarten kids—immature and childish.

We seated ourselves in the movie hall and Rohit got us popcorn and Coke. He sat between Moh and me. Honestly, I was nervous as hell and would have preferred to sit next to Moh, but I kind of liked my proximity to Rohit also. Soon, we were all engrossed in the movie; it was a mystery that kept us glued to our seats. After a while, I felt Rohit's arm snake its way behind my chair. Instantly, I stiffened. He turned towards me and whispered in my ear, his lips very close to my earlobes, 'It's okay. Relax, put your head against my arm and just enjoy the movie.'

Mesmerized and attracted like a plant to sunlight, I leaned against his arm. Almost immediately this unleashed a whole new world of sensations in me. I felt a tingling starting at the point of contact, going up to my head and running down my spine and legs. As I sat lost in this world, Rohit nudged me all too soon. The lights were coming on signalling that the movie was nearing the interval. I jerked up straight and looked guiltily at Moh, who was blissfully unaware of what was happening around her.

During the interval, Rohit got up and winked at me. I blushed and was glad that the lights were too dim for Moh to notice. He got us more Coke and nachos and sat down. Soon the lights dimmed and the movie started. Again, Rohit put his arm around the back of my chair, but this time I didn't lean. It had gotten too comfortable for my liking. He smiled but didn't push it, for which I was immensely grateful.

On our way back, Rohit and Moh dissected the movie and I was glad for this as I was in no condition to hold any conversation. As Rohit walked me to the gate of my house, he said, 'I'm leaving in two days and I want to keep in touch with you. I'm going to be back in six months and I hope you will keep yourself free for me then.' With this, he was gone.

It was raining. Rohit and I were running towards each other in slow motion, as it so often happens in the movies.

He held me by my waist and lifted me up, whirling me around effortlessly. I was wearing a short white diaphanous dress that swung around my hips, in sync with the flow of my open hair. As he put me down, we both lost our balance and, still holding each other, started rolling down a vale…

Thud! I rolled off my bed and landed on my back, which hurt. What a silly dream! Even in the dream I should have realized that it was only a dream for three reasons—for one, I never leave my hair open, second, I was not wearing my spectacles and third, but most important, a handsome chap like Rohit, who was always surrounded by the most attractive girls, had no business wasting his time on a mouse such as me.

6

I found myself thinking about Rohit often. I would catch myself daydreaming and with some effort force my thoughts back to my studies. I wanted to ace my exams and make Papa proud. I admired him so much and so desperately wanted to be an engineer like him. I wanted to be a civil engineer so that I could build bridges, roads and huge buildings. I always envisioned myself with a helmet, on a construction site, looking very important and commanding my team on various operations.

However, I was getting to see so little of Papa these days. The end of the fiscal year was nearing and he not only had to meet various production targets but also had this issue of agitating workers to deal with. Even though he was very senior, he was a very hands-on person. Pa had faced such situations many times before, and with his simplicity and honesty that so endeared him to all, had always managed to resolve issues amicably. In the three years in his current role for which he had been handpicked by the management, he had won many performance awards, for which he had always given credit to his team.

Fortunately, the final exams' preparations kept me

occupied. Moh and I mostly studied together. It was difficult to believe that Class XI was almost over.

As the exams ended, I was confident that I had done well. Like me, Moh too had done well, but I knew that while she was brilliant, she was also careless and a tad lazy. Even though this attitude would cost her marks, she did not care.

After the last exam, the four of us hung around at Coffee Express for a while. I reached home rather late. I found it difficult to settle down. Also, in the excitement of the exams getting over, I had lost my will to sleep even though that's what I had been craving for all this while! I logged on to my Facebook account and saw a friend request.

I was selective about the friends I liked to have and rejected most of the requests that came. But this one was different, oh so very different! It was from Rohit. Quickly, I saw his profile picture. Oh God! He looked incredibly hot dressed in a black T-shirt, ripped jeans and aviators.

It was a small thing perhaps and maybe I should not have read too much into it, but I was beside myself with joy. He'd actually not forgotten me! No sooner had I accepted the request the chat window opened. 'Hi!'

I quickly ran and bolted my bedroom door before typing, 'Hi!'

'So what is my gorgeous girl up to these days?' I was so glad that he couldn't see me; the colour creeping up my neck would have been very unbecoming. With trembling fingers I lied, 'Planning a movie for tomorrow.'

'Without me? Hope it is only with girls!'

'Yes, our usual gang.'

'I remember the movie we went for together. Do you?'

'Oh yes!' I typed. As if I could ever forget.

'Anu, you know what? I wish you were here. It is spring now, there are flowers everywhere and the weather is lovely. Time to be with loved ones.'

Anu… loved ones… I didn't know what to write back.

'Our exams got over today,' I replied stupidly.

'I know silly. Remember I have a sister who is in your class and is your best friend? Anu you are so innocent and adorable. I love that in you.'

By then, I had died and gone to heaven!

'Listen, your friend Amit was looking daggers at me the other day. Moh tells me he is a very good friend of yours. Is he only a friend or something more?'

After Sanjana, Rohit was the second one to hint at such a thing. And could Rohit possibly be jealous? My thoughts soared at the mere imagination of this.

'No such thing, Rohit. Amit is just an old family friend. Our fathers studied in the same school and now work in the same firm as well.'

'I sure hope so ☺. I don't like to have competition!'

I was flying high, high in the air.

'Gtg, Anu. It was great chatting with you. Gnite.'

I had just had the most divine experience of my life.

'Gnite Rohit.'

'Hugs and kisses, Anu! Bye!'

I was sure I had turned beetroot red. But something in me dared to type back.

'Same to you.'

I went to bed with dreamy eyes and lay awake for a long while before finally falling asleep.

It turned out to be an incredibly hot summer. The sun's rays were bright from the early hours of the morning. The afternoons were like a furnace. The streets were deserted and everything was still. Even the stray dogs grew languorous and were seen sleeping away the hot afternoons under the shade of trees. The shrapnel-like rays hit everything in sight, the air heated the tarred roads, which shimmered and sent shivering mirages in the air just above them.

As I'd expected, Papa was returning home later and later with every passing day, barely in time to join us for dinner. I wondered how it was possible for him to stand for hours on end in this sweltering heat in front of the molten metal on the shop floor. Even then, he would be his usual pleasant self and, over breakfast, ask me about my previous day's activities and also discuss the latest events with Mom. Mom headed the HR department at a large IT firm and was the perfect career woman—smart and focused. She was well read, extremely intelligent and had an opinion on most things—from the prices of vegetables, to corruption, sports and politics—and I knew that Pa was always interested in knowing her view on various subjects.

At my end, things soon settled into a comfortable summer vacation routine. I would spend the first half of the day going to my coaching classes and studying. I would meet Amit daily at these classes; we would discuss lectures, tests and exchange notes. Despite what Sanjana and Rohit had insinuated, I still saw Amit in the same light as before. He was great company and a helpful friend. I would spend the remaining day with my friends, watch TV and go swimming.

And then I would chat till late night with Rohit—his

comments were getting saucier and more intimate by the day. My ears would turn red at times with what he would write or imply, but after that first chat with him when I had replied boldly, I didn't respond to them. While at the surface I ignored most of his comments, secretly I relished them.

7

D-day came and the results were pretty much as expected. I had scored a winner, Amit was second and Moh was third. The three of us met at a coffee shop in the evening to celebrate our success.

Class XII began soon enough and we were very lucky to have gotten a great set of teachers. Our sports department organized a picnic cum trek for the next weekend. I was quite excited. When the day of the trip arrived, I woke up at an ungodly hour and after quickly getting ready, I left for school with Dad.

We all boarded the school bus, which left sharp at five in the morning. Amit sat next to me and smiled warmly. Seeing this, Sanjana's eyes danced in an, 'I told you so!' merriment. I gave her a severe look, which said 'SHUT UP!' I didn't want anything messing up my easygoing, comfortable friendship of years with Amit. There was a fair bit of singing, and as always we split into two groups for a good round of antakshari, each side spoiling for a good fight. Sanjana led one team and Amit led ours. Unlike the rest of us, Amit usually favoured old Hindi songs and we teased him mercilessly for that, which he took sportingly. In our class, he probably had the best voice.

Though Amit was very studious, he had many other interests as well. Apart from being the captain of the school cricket team, he was also actively involved in the English literary club. Though I was always picking up the class topper trophies, he was always being awarded 'all-rounder of the year' awards.

We set out on the trek at 10 am. The weather was perfect and having rained the night before, the sky was clear. We all started with great enthusiasm and soon fell into a rhythm. However, within no time Amit and his gang—Dev, Dhruv and Kabir—started walking right behind us, singing songs—really stupid love songs—and Amit was the loudest of them all.

It was annoying to see that Sanjana and Nandini were quite delighted with the attention and were giggling merrily, even turning back once or twice to smile at the boys, as if they needed any more encouragement. Moh thankfully was her calm self.

Around midday, we were exhausted. My legs hurt badly; I could feel the pain shooting from my heels all the way up. Because of the occasional drizzle, my shoes and indeed most of my track pants had become dirty and muddy. I thought of my comfortable, cosy room with crisp, clean sheets and felt even more miserable. Finally, drawing upon the last vestiges of my strength, I plodded on. Huffing and puffing, we reached the top in another half an hour. I felt dead.

But when I looked around, the view had me spellbound. It was worth all the pain that I had to endure and much more! It was so panoramic. It felt like heaven—I could see the nearby peaks, waterfalls and a stream gurgling close by. Around me were plants with wild flowers of all hues and trees bearing wild fruits.

I felt alive like never before. I sat with my eyes closed for a while, forgetting the group and the buzz around me, filling my being with the feel of the breeze and the sound of water running down the stream.

After a good lunch, we packed up and began our descent. Since we all knew, though no one mentioned it, that this was our last school picnic, we tried to make the most of it. Soon, I even forgot my irritation with Amit and his gang, and we all walked down together.

The momentum of our studies picked up immediately after we returned from the picnic. We too were conscious that at the end of year, we had our all-India board exams as well as competitive exams to take. Though I had merrily chatted with Rohit on Facebook all summer while he was in the US with the safety of the distance between us, it had taken me a great amount of will power to cut down on that temptation.

Moh would come over often to study with me or play badminton. That day after a good round of badminton, I ventured to the kitchen as I had offered to make Moh some bhelpuri, her favourite snack and my self-claimed area of expertise. Meanwhile, she took off to my room to read some new books I'd bought recently.

After mixing all the ingredients for the bhel—puffed rice, chopped onions, peanuts, sev etc. in a bowl—all that was left was to add the Imli Pichkoo sauce. I tried to do that with some flair, holding the bottle a fair bit away from the bowl and rotating it in a circle all the while aiming successfully and squirting it in the bowl. Just when I was almost done, I heard a sound behind my back which startled me. As I lost concentration, the Imli Pichkoo landed everywhere—on my hands, on the front of my tee and on the kitchen platform. Irritated, I turned towards the source of the disturbance and froze. Rohit was leaning against the doorframe and watching me with an amused expression on his face. I felt flustered—I must have been looking so untidy and like a complete idiot with the Imli Pichkoo all over my hands and clothes.

'Hi Ananya,' he said smoothly.

'Uh, hi!' I croaked back, and then cleared my throat. His sudden and unexpected appearance had a paralyzing effect on me. I suddenly felt very awkward and uncomfortable; the intimacy of our cyber world vanished in a second in the real world, or maybe, I was just a big coward.

'I have come to pick up Moh, could you please call her?' he asked amusedly, his eyes twinkling.

'Oh yes. Yes, of course,' I ran upstairs to my room, but was conscious of his slight laughter following me. I told Moh that Rohit had come to pick her up. 'Oh yes, I forgot to tell you. He's here for a couple of months for the research assignment he is doing under Papa before he goes back. While he's here, his elderly brother attitude is in full force!' Moh said with a smile. Oh what must have Rohit thought of me! My appearance had been no better than a child's.

'Meet me at the Barista near your school at 6 pm tomorrow– Rohit,' the SMS read. Shoot! I was really excited by the fact that he must have bothered to take my number from Moh and that he wanted to meet me again. Yipee!

At the given time, I was outside the coffee shop and luckily, I didn't have to wait long for Rohit. The minute he sat down, a waiter appeared. Usually, it would take us 5–10 minutes of gesturing to get any waiter's attention. But then, we didn't have Rohit's charisma and charm. I ordered a café latte and Rohit ordered an espresso. Oh! Everything about him was so sophisticated; we would all order frothy coffees, rich with cream and spoonfuls of sugar. Rohit was different.

'So Ananya, tell me this. Have you been trying to avoid me? I can almost see you logging out when I'm online and you haven't even replied to some of my e-mails. What is it? You don't like me anymore or is to do with that Amit?' he asked, staring into my eyes with soul-melting intensity.

I didn't know what to say or do. Yes, I was cutting down on my time spent online with him but that was only because he was becoming a larger-than-life presence in my life and I felt inadequate to deal with it, not because of the other reason as he alleged. Also, I was trying my best to not lose my focus on my studies.

'No, Rohit. Nothing like that. I have just been very busy with my studies.'

I wanted to add, 'I like you, like you very much. In fact more than all my other friends!' but the words didn't come. However, the force of my feelings hit me like a blast and left me reeling.

'I'm glad to hear that. But I have come to collect all the hugs and kisses you have been promising me.' The intensity in his eyes was replaced by something else, part mischief and part something that I couldn't name.

I tipped my head down, too embarrassed at my earlier boldness.

'So you are a paper tiger, I can see that.'

'Hey, don't look so serious. I was just kidding. Want to go for a walk?' he had been teasing me and was laughing openly now. He looked so gorgeous that my heart stopped beating.

Feeling silly and self-conscious, I nodded.

Then, setting down his cup, leaving enough money to cover the bill and a healthy tip (which was again unthinkable for my friends) and holding my hand, he guided me out of the coffee shop. He drove around for a while and then stopped at a park.

By now the sun had set and the last of the joggers and mothers with squealing children were in the process of going home. Hand in hand, we went into the park and started walking aimlessly. After five minutes, Rohit pulled off the scrunchie holding my ponytail and said he liked my hair loose. I shivered at his touch and he asked me if I was cold. To hide my nervousness I nodded a yes. He shrugged off his jacket and covered me with it. The touch of his hands, the intimacy of the action had me almost swooning; it took a lot of effort to place one foot in front of the other. I blushed in embarrassment when I realized that I must look so gauche and unsophisticated to him.

8

The next couple of days were a flurry of excitement. Papa was promoted in his firm and we moved into a new house, a charming old bungalow in a very posh part of Pune. All this happening on the heels of me topping Class XI—it was as if Christmas and Diwali had come together. We decided to throw a huge party to celebrate our collective success.

The next fortnight saw preparations on a war scale at home. My main contribution to the party was mostly to stay out of Mom and Amma's way. Amma had been my nanny when I was young and had stayed on even after I grew up. Now she mainly did odd jobs around the house and supervised the domestic help.

I heard Ma call out for me. I ran downstairs and my jaw fell open when I saw her. I had always known she was pretty but today she looked regal. Her hair cascaded all the way down to her waist and she was wearing a turquoise green chiffon saree with a gold border and a sleeveless blouse. As I stood gaping at her, Papa came out of the room and surprised me even more. It was as if I was looking at my parents for the first time! He looked dashing in a full-sleeved white shirt and a blue silk tie. As they stood next to each other and smiled, they looked made for each other and so much in love. The clothes which Ma had gotten stitched for me were very pretty—a pink ghagra-choli which had a sheer dupatta with silver sequins.

The first to arrive were Nandini and Sanjana. When Sanjana saw me, she slowly tipped her head to one side, raised an eyebrow and, smiling, said in the most dramatic manner, 'My, my! Someone is looking very hot today. I can imagine dozens of guys swooning at your feet!' Oh, Sanjana's thinking horizon was limited only to boys. I wanted to give her a good kick, but my ghagra prevented me from indulging in this antic, so I threw a scowl in her direction instead which said, 'Buzz off!'

I saw Moh walking in. And with Rohit! He looked so sophisticated, dressed all in black. I felt my throat go dry—no one had the right to be so good looking, like an apparition of a Greek God come to earth. I suddenly felt light-headed. I shook my head in an attempt to clear it. 'Hi! Ananya. How have you been?' he asked me, cool as a cucumber. I stared at him open-mouthed and I noticed the mischievous twinkle in his eyes. But what does one do if God suddenly decides to make an appearance? I focused on Moh. Just looking at her calmed me down. I was able to gather my wits and trying to match his tone, I greeted Rohit as coolly as possible. He said 'Congratulations Ananya, well done,' clasping my hands briefly but firmly. I felt a tingling going up my arm and up my brain threatening to cause a short circuit in all my nerves. I saw something flash in Rohit's eyes too but whatever it was, it was gone in a moment. Maybe it was my just my imagination.

Pa called me just then and I decided to ignore Rohit all evening lest someone guess my feelings toward him. I decided to make some excuse later. Papa introduced me to his colleagues with pride and spoke about my excellent results. Just then I saw Amit walk in with his parents. I was so happy to see him! It was like being in my safety zone again.

'So, Ananya continues to beat Amit in the exams!' and with a warm smile, Uncle congratulated me on my results.

Amit was dressed smartly in a white full-sleeved shirt and jeans. 'It is only because I let her,' he added good-humouredly after greeting Papa politely. Uncle and Pa went back a long way and their friendship was based on mutual respect and admiration.

As Papa led Uncle towards the drinks and Mom took Aunty to her group and I chatted merrily with Amit I felt something searing into my back. I turned around and saw a pair of dark, intense eyes looking at me which didn't look away. Rohit stood surrounded by a throng of boys and his eyes looked straight at me above their heads. Though the difference in their ages would not have been more than 5–6 years, it seemed like a generation gap as Rohit had a certain maturity about him. Pulled by a gravitational force towards him, I cut short my conversation with Amit and herded him towards that group. At a subconscious level I registered that Amit was probably the bridge between these two generations— younger in years than Rohit but more mature than boys his age. I could make out bits of conversation around Rohit. These were boys who wanted tips on how to crack the IIT, go to the US, etcetera. After a round of quick introductions and managing to avoid looking into Rohit's eyes directly, I quickly left Amit with the group. I walked back to my group of friends relieved to be outside Rohit's eye contact, though I felt a tad guilty at having dumped Amit like that within minutes of his arrival.

Some of my school friends were visiting our house for the first time and wanted to see it. I showed them around with immense pride, reserving my room for the last. We had a clear view of the party scene from my window. And then I saw *him*. He was lounging against the garden wall, nursing a drink; he wore a hooded expression. He was in my direct line of vision. By now the house tour was complete and I told the girls to go join the party, I would be back in a moment.

I went to my dressing mirror and had a good look at myself. My friends always told me that I would look better without my spectacles and that I should start wearing contact lenses. However, so far, I had not heeded their advice. I slowly took off my glasses and my reflection blurred. I went back to the window. I could see his silhouette. I stood rooted to the spot, willing him to look at me.

Suddenly he looked up and I think, in my direction. But without my glasses, I couldn't be sure. Damn! Plus, suddenly I was not very comfortable being caught staring. I pulled the curtain back and walked out of the room.

'You will need your glasses to see clearly Ananya,' Amit was standing just outside my room. Oh my God! For how long had he been watching me?! I suddenly felt uncomfortable and edgy as if his words had another meaning, a double meaning, or maybe I was being overly sensitive. 'Oh yes,' I said, flustered. 'Did you want anything?' 'Ananya, your father is looking for you. He asked me to call you.' But a mask had slipped over his face even as he said this.

'Okay, thanks. I was going anyway.' However, heeding his earlier words I went to my room and picked up my glasses.

Amit left soon after, despite my parents' protests, as Uncle had an early flight to catch the next day. Just then a voice murmured close to my ears, 'Getting bored, Ananya?' I didn't need to turn around to find out the owner of this deep, sexy voice, but the shock of the moment led to goose pimples all over my arms.

'The weather is perfect for a drive. Let us go for a spin.'

I looked up at the sky. Swollen rainclouds were moving in from the west, slicing the sky in half—midnight blue studded with stars on one side and a dark, angry gray rumbling on the other.

'Will Moh also come? Let me check with Mom.'

'No, Moh will not come. And no, you will not check with your Mom. You are almost 18. Remember Ananya, you are a big girl now; you don't need to go running to your parents for every small thing. We will be back before anyone finds out that you are missing. Besides, I have bought something for you. Don't you want to see it?'

With the devil urging me on, I said yes. And it had nothing to do with the gift he had got.

Rohit kept the car windows rolled down. The cool and heavy air was suspended with raindrops. There was a certain promise of things to come. But the silence in the car was awkward; I kept knotting and unknotting the corner of the dupatta in my hand, trying to find my composure.

I secreted a glance at Rohit. Unlike me he looked relaxed, the wind ruffling his hair softly. However, I couldn't relax, I wanted to go back. Suddenly some big raindrops plopped on the windscreen of the car. Rohit looked outside, pressed a button, and rolled the windows up.

I occupied myself with the sound of the drops against the car's window. The rain was falling so hard and so fast now that I couldn't even make out where we were going. I felt the car slowing down; I looked at Rohit with questioning eyes. He smiled at me, a warm tender smile. The car stopped. Time stopped too.

'Has anyone ever told you how beautiful you are?' Rohit stroked my cheek with the back of his hand. Panicking, I looked outside. It was a curtain of steel all around. We felt cut off from the entire outside world, even cut off from reality, ensconced in our private world.

'Close your eyes.'

I did.

'Now open them slowly.'

Just then lightning zigzagged across the sky and in that flash of a second I saw a round bottle of cobalt blue in his hand.

'I bought this perfume for you. It has the essence of spring flowers and reminded me of you.'

'Let me apply it for you.'

'No Rohit. I mean thanks for the nice gift, but I will use it later.'

'Ananya, don't be so uptight. Just relax. You trust me, don't you?'

Sheets of rain sluiced over the windows; thunder was alive in the distance.

I felt a cool spray of perfume on the heated skin of my wrist and then a thumb running in circles over the spot. My eyes grew heavy, lids half-closed. I felt a cool spray behind my ear lobe followed by a feather-light massage. Tenderly he folded my dupatta and kept it in my lap. His hands moved to the back of my neck slowly massaging away the tension there. A swift current was carrying me away and slowly I was getting pulled under.

Suddenly I felt a warm breath fan my face. My eyes fluttered open. I saw his face slowly tip forward and the intensity of the emotions in his eyes hypnotized me. I knew he was going to kiss me. From somewhere, Sanjana's shy laugh echoed in my head when she had described her first kiss with Luv to us. Rohit's lips were on mine now and somehow that paralyzed me into staying absolutely still. Then a bizarre thought crossed my mind—no, Rohit's lips were not chapped! That was the last coherent thought I was to have for a long while.

My hands moved to encircle his neck, pulling him even closer. The kiss was everything I had thought it would be and much more. I felt as if the earth had stopped spinning on its axis, as if the whole universe had come to a standstill. I felt as if I was transported to another world, a world so magical that it was impossible to describe it. I felt as if the heavens had opened and were luring me in. I had no idea how long the kiss went on, but then too soon, Rohit was pulling away. As I slowly surfaced from under, disappointment must have been clear on my face. Placing the dupatta back on me, he said, 'Kiddo, we are already very late. I don't want you to get into trouble with your parents.' At that moment I didn't care about anyone or anything else in the world, not even the consequence of reaching home late. I suddenly felt cold and yes, even irritable. I had been so comfortable in the lethargy of drowning, I had not wanted to surface to reality.

But the moment passed, I sighed—Rohit was right. Luckily,

when we reached home Mom was busy taking care of her guests while tackling the additional complication of rain, so I was able to sneak in unnoticed.

As I lay in bed that night, I thought of my first kiss and was so glad that it had been with Rohit. He made it so perfect for me. He was such a sophisticated, mature guy and was extremely good looking to boot. As a deep yawn escaped me, I switched off the lamp, turned on to my side and clutched the pillow. Strangely, my mind was filled with one thought that didn't let go of me even with closed eyes. Suddenly, my eyes flew open. I put on the lamp and tried to hold that fleeting thought. The state in which I had been neither awake nor yet asleep, had freed my subconscious, which registered the fact that my feelings for Rohit transcended mere attraction. Oh crap! I was head over heels in love with him.

9

After Rohit happened to me, I caught myself smiling for no reason and hardly paid attention to what was being taught in class. I guess it was fortunate that I was quite ahead of the class and so I was comfortably able to handle the various assignments and class tests.

I was now beginning to understand what drug addicts must feel like. Like them, I too looked forward to my daily dose of Rohit with desperation. I was getting addicted to him and the sensations that his touch unleashed made me restless to no end. I admitted to myself that I was getting obsessed.It was five days since Rohit had first kissed me and since then I had cut down the time spent with my friends and probably, even neglected some. Especially Amit. Something seemed to have come over him since the day of the party—a day when, even if I were to admit it to myself, I had acted as less than a perfect host. Something uncomfortable seemed to be hanging between us and we barely spoke these days. However, I didn't bother much about it, we were old buddies after all, I was sure it would work out by itself soon enough. Right now, I was flying, flying high…

I also suddenly found myself visiting Moh's house more

often than ever before. Of course, we studied together at those times and no, it had nothing to do with the fact that Rohit lived there. Anyway, most of the time, he would be out. In fact the last time I had seen him, he was going somewhere with Aditi. Yes the same Aditi who though a class duffer, was quite a looker. Not only that, she probably spent more on makeup, dresses and shoes than the four of us put together. Even Sanjana, who was the most fashion-savvy in our group, didn't use any makeup. Aditi was unbelievably self-conscious about her looks. Needless to say, she was very popular with the boys and equally unpopular with the girls, especially with the four of us. She had her circle of male admirers and was quite famous for her many 'escapades'.

Moh had mentioned earlier that Rohit and Aditi were good friends, though she was not exactly sure how their friendship had come about. But I knew, it was just two people—two extremely good looking people—coming together. Knowing is one thing, liking it is another. The thought of them together sent a shaft of pain through me. The last time I saw her at Moh's with Rohit, she was wearing a short and figure-hugging pale yellow dress with matching earrings, bracelet and sandals. Seeing her go out with Rohit, I was aware of the painful contrast between my plain looks and her glamour. Rohit smiled and waved at us before going off even as Aditi totally ignored us. I thought of my kiss with Rohit and was a bit confused at his behaviour. I wanted to know what was going on. But would that be appropriate; would that be assuming too much? Well, if he could question me about Amit, then I surely had the right to quiz him about Aditi the witch!

Moh always studied with her iPod blasting music in her ears. This was a blessing as it allowed me to pace up and down, reading the tough portions aloud to myself. I was doing exactly that—reading out portions from my chemistry book and trying to memorize some tough equations in inorganic chemistry when Rohit walked in. Suddenly the room and everything in it shrunk. I stood open-mouthed, mid-equation, all the equations fleeing my mind.

'Hi girls! How goes it? I was just going to make myself some coffee and wondered if you girls would like some as well.'

Oh! Why was Rohit home today of all days? He was never there on those days when I played badminton scintillatingly, the one thing at which I was better than Moh. Nor was he ever there when I played chess with Uncle, probably looking sophisticated. But he had to be there today when I was walking up and down chanting chemistry equations, looking and sounding dim-witted.

Moh took off her headphones and said, 'What?' When Rohit repeated the question, she said, 'Oh yeah, sure. I could do with a cup of coffee and a break.' She stretched, got up and left the room to freshen up. Rohit shot me a questioning glance. I just about managed to nod mutely. He smiled at me and said, 'You know, you looked damn cute studying like that.' I tugged at my T-shirt and looked down. I couldn't come up with any appropriate response as my tongue seemed glued to the bottom of my mouth. Instead I said awkwardly, 'Hey Rohit, do you like Aditi? You seem to be spending an awful lot of time with her.' There it was, the green-eyed monster bared for all to see. I closed my eyes, I would not have been able to bear it if Rohit had chosen to laugh at me now.

'Anu, open your eyes,' he said softly. 'Look at me. Aditi is just a friend, that too not a very close or good one. For me, it is only you. However, since you are busy with your studies, sometimes I like to go out with my other friends as well.'

I smiled sheepishly, though not unlike a child caught eating more toffees than allowed, but at the same time, I felt infinitely better at having gotten the air cleared. The issue had been a thorn in my side for a while now.

Luckily Moh came back just then and Rohit disappeared to get us coffee.

In a while, he returned with three cups of coffee. 'Do you girls need help with any subject?' he asked.

Moh and I had made a list of doubts that we wanted to clarify with our teachers. Moh quickly went and fetched it. Rohit spent the next hour or so patiently answering our questions and clearing our doubts. I was quite impressed by his conceptual clarity and depth of knowledge. 'Okay girls, enough for today,' he said, glancing at his watch. He had answered most of our questions already. He asked us to hand over our empty cups. As he moved forward to take my cup, his fingers touched mine and stayed there for a while. To my delight, his touch felt wonderful. And then, just like that, he was gone.

10

'I will pick you up Friday evening from your coaching class. Will take you shopping,' read the SMS. Unlike some of my friends I was not a shopping aficionado, but I was very excited at the prospect of meeting Rohit again.

I was at Moh's place when I received this SMS. Moh's house had become my sanctuary and I would end up there on most evenings when I didn't have my coaching classes especially with both Ma and Pa working late hours these days. Even when Moh was out, I would have a cup of evening tea with Uncle and Aunty and then spend some time playing chess with Uncle. I knew that Moh's parents were fond of me and I had always considered her place as my second home.

Gollum was just not letting up. Today, we'd been doing trigonometry and he had grilled us so much that it was a big relief when the two-hour class was over. I handed over the assignment to him and peeped out of the window—the sun had dipped and the birds were creating a racket in the excitement of returning home after a day's hard work. I slung my backpack over my shoulder and walked down the stairs with Amit, discussing some particularly tough problems from Loney's trigonometry book, a book which was considered the

Bible for this subject. Some sort of normalcy had returned between Amit and me. At the bottom of the stairs, as I finally shut the book feeling mentally exhausted, two things happened at once. Amit said, 'Coffee?' and Rohit called out from his car, 'Ananya, done? Let's go.'

Oh my God! Rohit was to take me shopping today. Hours of trigonometry had wiped it clean from my memory. Rohit was reversing the car, I was thankful for a few moments to compose myself.

'I'm sorry, Amit, I had promised him. I have got to go,' I said as I heard the car hooting impatiently.

I ran to the car before it attracted more attention as many students were looking our way already.

'So what do you want me to buy for you?' Rohit asked. 'Or are you hungry, Anu? Would you like to eat something first?'

'I'm okay. I'm not hungry. And Rohit I cannot let you buy anything for me. Maybe we could just go to a coffee shop.'

'Anu, you take things too seriously. Just chill.'

I closed my eyes and tried to relax against the car seat. The car was stopping—I must have dozed off, the stress of the long day plus the car AC had conspired towards that. Rohit smoothly parked the car, smiled and said, 'Okay, here we are! Let's go.'

Oh! The boutique we went to was so out of my league. It only had designer labels; I walked around the place in a daze. Each outfit was lovelier than the other and each one, so not me. Sanjana would have just loved this place.

'Look for something in red,' he said.

I walked around the store on rubber legs and finally selected a red T-shirt. As I turned to show it to him, I saw he was admiring a red dress.

'Anu, come here,' he took the red T-shirt without even giving it the benefit of a glance and handed it over to one of the boutique assistants. He placed the dress against my shoulders and said, 'Hold it.' He stepped back and looked at me critically.

'Anu, could you go and change?' Rohit nudged me into the changing room.

I went to the changing room and looked at the dress. It was an exquisite red satin-silk, halter-neck evening dress with small black flowers on it, whose density grew from the top to the bottom. I gaped at the price tag—it was an exorbitant amount. We would not buy it, but to please Rohit I would just wear it and show it to him once. I took off my jeans and T-shirt and looked at myself in the full-length mirror. I would never be able to carry this off, this dress needed curves and it needed guts, both of which—I was honest enough to admit— I lacked. Still, I had no choice. I pulled the dress over my head, smoothed it down, tied the knot behind my neck and zipped it up at the side.

Oh no! My white cotton bra was peeping from everywhere—from the front, from the sides and from the back and taking away the entire beauty of the dress. I couldn't go out like this. Rohit's, 'Ananya, are you done?' spurred me into action. I made up my mind; maybe this dress was to be worn without a bra. I quickly took off the dress, took off my bra, and slipped the dress back on.

As I finished pulling the zipper up and looked in the mirror, I couldn't believe what I saw. This was not me! The girl in the mirror suddenly had curves and almost looked glamorous. I shook my head and looked closely. She was also half-naked, what with the plunging neckline, a bare back and the flare of the dress ending a few inches above the knees.

I immediately wanted to change back into my jeans and T-shirt. 'Are you coming out or should I come in?' Rohit said. I was sure that he was joking, but since the changing room only had a curtain and not a door, I didn't want to risk the second option and quickly stepped out.

Rohit stood still when he saw me and didn't react at all. I was feeling so unsure that I wanted to duck back in the changing room when I saw him smile, a beautiful warm smile which lit up his eyes. 'Why Ananya, you look like a princess. I could look at you like this forever. You are looking beautiful beyond imagination. Come closer.'

I walked towards him but was not able to meet his eyes. I felt hot all over.

'Should I go and change now?' I asked.

'Na, keep this on, come with me for dinner in this.'

'Rohit I cannot go out like this. I feel very uncomfortable, please understand.' There was a note of desperation in my voice which probably reached him.

'Okay. Could you please help her out?' Rohit requested the boutique assistant very courteously, with equal amounts of charm. 'Of course sir.' She went into a tizzy and I almost pitied her.

A couple of minutes later she surfaced with a matching tube top in black and handed it to me.

With the tube inside the dress, I felt immensely more comfortable and it didn't take away from the smartness of the dress as well. A win-win situation. 'Comfortable now?' Rohit teased me with twinkling eyes.

'But Rohit, it is way too expensive.'

'Shh, let me worry about that okay? You go and pick up your bag.'

He flashed his credit card at the counter and asked the assistant to pack the clothes I had been wearing.

Rohit then took me to a shoe store and insisted that I buy matching sandals, since my sneakers definitely didn't go with the dress. This time I didn't protest. The black gladiators with heels and just a dash of red added immensely to the glamour of the outfit. Rohit pulled out a tie from the car dashboard and put it on before starting the car. I wondered where we were going next. However, Rohit refused to satisfy my curiosity. Just a few minutes later, I saw the car pulling up in front of the city's most exclusive five-star hotel. Oh no! We were not going there!

The car glided smoothly into the porch and before I could say or do anything, a smartly dressed and turbaned doorman opened the door. Rohit was at my side before I could even get out. He linked his hand with mine and took me smoothly inside the hotel. The high ceiling, sparking chandeliers, smartly dressed men and gorgeous women moving about, sounds of tinkling laughter from one corner and clinking glasses from another, a mellow tune being played on the piano and the world's most handsome and caring guy at my side—I felt like a princess! I had never been happier or more pampered in my life.

'This way, Ananya.' The restaurant was on the first floor and we chose to walk up. We suddenly came upon a huge mirror in gilded frame at the end of the flight of the stairs. I stopped short at the reflection staring back at me—Rohit and I standing side by side. He was standing next to me in a black formal shirt and trousers teamed with a red silk tie and I was standing next to him in my new red dress with tiny black flowers printed on it. Gosh, suddenly I realized we were even perfectly colour coordinated. I didn't know whether it was a coincidence or intentional. Whatever it was, the effect was mindblowing.

Rohit too seemed affected by the moment. He put his arms around me and in the mirror I saw him smile at me. I took a mental snapshot of the mirror with its gilded frame and the reflection in it, knowing that I would preserve it forever and take it out of the folds of my memories to look at whenever I missed Rohit.

'Reservation for two in the name of Rohit Singh.'

'This way please,' the waiter guided us to a table in the corner partly shielded from view by a huge flower decoration made with orchids. The table had a long slim lit candle in an old fashioned wrought iron stand throwing a soft mellow light. A candlelight dinner with the most handsome guy in the world!

Nothing in life had felt so good. Nothing could be better. Rohit covered my hands with his and looked deep into my eyes, 'Did you know that you are the most beautiful girl in the whole world?' My eyes misted as I looked up at him. 'Rohit, I love you,' I blurted out in the most unsophisticated manner. But I didn't regret it. Rohit's hands, which were stroking the back of my hands, stopped and held my hands tightly, 'Ananya, this is huge. I'm not sure if I deserve it, but thanks.'

He was about to say something more, but the waiter arrived just then and Rohit gave our order.

'What are your plans after IIT?'

'I want to be a civil engineer. Our country's infrastructure is in a very bad shape and is a big roadblock to our progress. I want to contribute in building our country's infrastructure—roads, buildings, bridges—everything,' I said passionately.

'Don't be in a hurry to take up a job. Why don't you think about coming to the US after your graduation? There are a lot of opportunities there, lot more than in India. I would be there too and could help you out.'

Put like that, the US suddenly seemed like a great option. However, only a fraction of the things we talked about and only a little of what we ate registered in my mind. My mind was like a sponge full of happiness not able to take in anything more.

Halfway home, I realized that I couldn't possibly go home in this dress. 'Rohit, I need to change.'

'I understand. I will pull up in a dark lane and you can change there.'

'See this is deserted enough, you can change in the back seat,' Rohit said pulling up the car.

'I'm going out, let me know once you are done.'

I had to manage all sorts of contortions to change my dress sitting in the back seat of the car. I managed to knock my elbows several times against the car door and my knees against the floor and let out a yelp each time. I was so not going to do this ever again in my life.

The car pulled up outside my home.

'Did you enjoy yourself?'

'Rohit, I don't know how to thank you. You made me feel so special, I will never forget this evening.'

'There will be many more such evenings, love. It's getting late, you need to go now. See ya soon.' Rohit gave me a light peck on the cheek and drove off into the night. I stood looking at the car till the tail lights were two red dots in the distance and then couldn't be seen anymore.

The whole evening had felt surreal. As soon as he left I pinched myself to check that I wasn't dreaming. Suddenly conscious of how late it was, I opened the gate and crept inside. Luckily Mom's car was not there.

'Arre Beta, why are you so late today?' Of course I still had to answer Amma, our house sentinel.

'Today there was an extra class,' I made up on the spot, feeling my nose grow longer like Pinnochio's. I almost touched it. 'Where is Papa?'

'Sahib was asking about you. He just had his dinner and has gone up. Memsaab will be back late, she's asked you to have your dinner and go to sleep.'

'Hello, Pa. Sorry I got late. There was an extra class today,' I said to him as I entered his room after dinner. The nose grew longer.

'It's fine, Anu. You are looking tired. Have you had your dinner?'

'Yes Pa, I have eaten. Good night,' I said hugging him.

11

I was increasingly finding my attention wavering in the middle of my studies to dwell upon 'certain' pleasant thoughts. The scenes from the evening spent with Rohit—when he took me shopping and then dinner—kept replaying in my mind. I didn't even try to banish them. In fact, I indulged in the pleasure of such warm memories.

My phone received an SMS: 'Will pick you up tomorrow evening from home. Be ready at 6.'

'Okay, see ya.'

The next day, I dressed with extra care. I took out a white halter-neck top and teamed it with a light green tube top and olive green trousers instead of my usual jeans. I stood in front of the mirror and slowly pirouetted. I was pleased at the effect. Regular badminton and swimming meant that I had well-toned arms, which were highlighted by the halter top; the attire had a very smart look to it.

I was cognizant of the change that was taking place in me. Before, I would not pay any attention to my looks, but now I was taking more care about my appearance. I would brush my hair longer, use lip gloss and dress more smartly. I even paid a visit to a horrendously expensive parlour (which ate up my year's book budget) and suffered various female agonies! I wore a jacket on top and left. I couldn't wait to see Rohit.

I was rewarded instantly by a smile from him. He looked me up and down and whistled.

'Hey, Ananya, you look very different today,' he said softly. 'Give me your jacket, you look better without it.'

We had driven to a park. As we started walking together, he pulled my hair free of the band. A small, involuntary sigh escaped my lips. Today he took his time running his hands on the nape of my neck, massaging the bare skin on my shoulders and playing with my hair. I couldn't focus on my walk. Somehow, my arms snaked around his waist and I held on to it for support as we walked and as he continued stroking me, his hands now moving down my spine and creating a riot of sensations. And to add to that, I was getting intoxicated on the fragrance of the night flowers in full blossom.

Just before dropping me back home, Rohit said that he'd bought movie tickets for tomorrow, but this time only for the two of us. While I was excited, I also knew this could turn into a sticky situation. What excuse would I give my parents as it being a Sunday, they would be home?

Anyway, the day of the 'movie date' arrived. Sanjana often joked that the only reason couples went to movies was to make out but I knew we weren't like that. Our relationship was very special and romantic, and I was quite sure he felt that way too. I was almost becoming a pro at lying. While I told my parents that I was going out for a movie with Moh and her brother, I told Moh that I was going out with Mummy and Papa for lunch and would be back late evening.

When Rohit's car drew up at our gate, I was already standing outside waiting for him.

Once we were seated in the theatre, Rohit got me my favourite caramel popcorn and cold drink. The movie started— it was a mindless one, an action flick. After a while, Rohit put his hand around the back of my chair and started playing with my hair. I turned to look at him—his face glorious in the silvery blue light reflecting off the movie screen—and he smiled at me. How I loved the feel of his fingers. Then he started stroking the sensitive area of my neck, pulling and tugging at my ear lobes, moving his fingers in an erratic rhythm, up and down my back, sending the most delightful sensations flooding through my blood stream. My eyes were shut in pure ecstasy and just when I thought I couldn't take any more, Rohit's hand slipped under my top.

The feel of his hands against the skin of my back sent shock waves through me and my eyes flew open. Sensing my reaction, he turned towards me with such love and then planted a tender kiss on my lips. While kissing me, his hands pulled down my bra strap and he began massaging my naked shoulder. On the screen in front of us, the hero was chasing the film's villains. Rohit and I were in our own world and fortunately, the theatre was almost empty. Rohit's hands slid down my back once more and he unhooked my bra. My blood was a simmer with an unexplainable emotion. I was putty in his hands, which moved freely up and down my back, sometimes feather light, sometimes pressing.

Then his hand snaked around and he touched my left breast. I stopped breathing. I shut my eyes, leaned back against his hand, giving in to the pleasure of wild sensations coursing through my body. I had given up all pretence of watching the movie. I was totally unaware of the passage of time, till he withdrew his hands. I felt my body tense, suddenly realizing for the first time how cold the hall was because of the air conditioning. I opened my eyes to protest, but saw that the movie credits were rolling. The theatre lights were slowly brightening. I panicked and, looking down at myself, saw that my clothes were crumpled and my bra undone. I quickly pushed the straps up my shoulders, but my hands were shaking so much that try as I might, I was not able to hook my bra. Rohit gently pushed my hands aside and in one deft movement hooked it. I turned to him with a grateful smile and gave him my hand to hold which was still shaking. By now, the cinema hall was lit with a depressing yellow light and four EXIT signs in red were shining brightly, guiding us to the door. Oh Sanjana was so right! Couples did come to the movies to make out. Ha-ha!

As we came out of the hall, I blinked against the harsh sunlight trying to adjust my vision. This action also brought me back to the real world, though the magic of what had happened inside the theatre was to stay with me. In the car Rohit turned towards me and with the most mischievous twinkle in his eyes asked, 'So did you enjoy the movie?' I wished I could say something smart in response; wished I could exchange an easy, charming, light-hearted banter with him; wished I knew how to flirt in a sophisticated manner; wished I was just a little bit like Sanjana or maybe even a wee bit like that despicable Aditi. Instead I was like a pre-schooler standing in front of the school principal desperately wanting to make an impression, aware that it was critical for securing admission, but not knowing how to. The child then resorts to looking down at some invisible speck of dust on his shiny shoes and busies himself clenching and unclenching his hands. That is exactly what I did. Also, at this point I was feeling a wee bit uncomfortable at what had happened in the theatre. So I just nodded a mute yes. As he dropped me home, he cupped my face in his hands and pulling me closer, nestled his nose next to mine. Just that. So innocent, so tender. But as I felt his warm breath fanning my cheeks, I inhaled him and felt my heart in my throat, beating at full speed. As I got out of the car, Rohit drove away leaving me with the small amount of sanity I had managed to gather on our drive back home.

12

As it was the year of the board exams, our class struggled with the extra assignments and class tests.

Though I was still coming first, the fact that Amit had narrowed the gap caused me no small amount of dismay, especially since we had almost stopped pretending to be friends or rather Amit had stopped. All this daydreaming and spending time with Rohit was not doing my studies any good. I had even bunked a couple of coaching classes to be with Rohit, something I would have never even considered earlier.

Once Rohit left, I would leave no stone unturned to get my lead back. On another front, I was facing increasing negative vibes from Aditi. One day as I walked past her, she hissed at me, 'Boys don't make passes at girls who wear glasses.' It was surprising, but her comments could still rankle me.

There was less than a week left for Rohit to leave for the US and time was running out like sand through a sieve. I had not seen him since the day of the movie. I went to Moh's house a couple of times hoping to see him but he was out each time. There must be a valid reason for this, must be his project. Moh had mentioned earlier in passing that Rohit had to wrap up his research project as his deadline was approaching.

I stared at the mobile phone for the nth time, willing it to ring. A phone that had its own distinct personality and was never quiet, refused to comply with my wishes today. 'I'm not going to let this bother me,' I told myself firmly and went to the study table. But less than a chapter and half an hour later, I was back to it. Maybe I had put it on silent mode by mistake and there might be missed calls.

I stared at the passive blank screen.

'Should I call him?' I thought and almost dialled his number a couple of times, but then stopped. 'He'll think I'm desperate or something. Maybe I will go to Moh's house again,' I thought. 'Even if Rohit isn't there, I can play badminton with Moh.' Just thinking about Moh cheered me up. No sooner had I made up my mind, the phone decided to ring. I dived at the bed where I'd tossed the phone in disgust. 'Rohit calling' flashed on the screen. 'Hold on a second, will you?' I dashed across the room and bolted the door. 'How are you?' I whispered in relief.

'I've missed you so much in the past few days, but didn't get a chance to contact you. How have been Anu?' Rohit's voice was so warm, so caressing that I collapsed on the bed, clutching the phone.

'Fine… I have missed you Rohit,' I croaked.

'Oh baby, I know. Moh suspects something is amiss and that's why I had to act cool. I know how possessive she can get about you and if she smells a rat, she'll tell our parents. That's why I kept my distance from you.' As I heard his explanation, I could feel the knots in my stomach start to ease. He continued, 'Nobody will be at home tomorrow. Everyone is attending the engagement of the daughter of my dad's colleague. I have excused myself from the boring, day-long function. Why don't you come over tomorrow to my house at two-ish? It will be our last chance to have some time to ourselves before I leave.'

Another chance to meet Rohit! Tomorrow was Saturday, which meant no school. I was free.

'Yes,' I replied.

'Great, look forward to seeing you,' Rohit said before disconnecting. I kept saying 'I love you' and kept kissing the phone long after that!

However, the prospect of meeting Rohit at his home when nobody was there, gave me an overwhelming feeling of restlessness—one which made me feel more lost and confused than I had ever felt in my life. Though I was impatient to meet him, a worm of uncertainty wriggled in the corner of my mind. The thing was that, till now, whenever I had met Rohit, it was in a public place—either at a coffee shop or the park or the movie theatre. And now alone?! That too in his house!

When I got up the next day, I was still unsure of my decision. Of course I knew Rohit well and I would only be going to Moh's house, which I had visited a zillion times, but still…

I was not sure how to deal with this. In the past, if I wanted a solution to any problem or was confused about something, I would discuss it with my best friend, my confidante Moh. Unlike some of my friends who could discuss anything under the sky with their mothers including stuff about their boyfriends, I had never been that close to Mom. I liked her well enough and my friends thought she was very cool, being so high up the corporate ladder and very pretty. She even took a fair level of interest in my studies, but she was not a very touchy-feely person and I somehow never felt comfortable enough to breach the private space around her. Probably the demands of her job left very little time for creating an effective bond between us.

But this time, consulting Moh was out of question. Anyway, given the nature of the subject and the wisdom required to deal with it, I knew that Sanjana was just the right person. I sent her an SMS: 'Need to discuss something urgently. Are you free now? Quick chat?' I sat holding the phone and within seconds got her reply, 'Sure, come over.'

Quickly, I hopped into an auto rickshaw and gave him the address. How much I had changed in the last month or so! I mused about my sudden and unexpected friendship with my best friend's brother. To be honest, I was extremely flattered by Rohit's interest in me.

I was jolted back into the present by the auto driver asking me for the fare. I quickly paid him and, as I reached the gate of Sanjana's house, she came running out. I could see she was very curious and I guess probably secretly happy that I had come to discuss something important with her instead of with Moh, as was the case usually. Once inside, she asked me, 'So what is it? Tell me fast!'

Now that I was there, my mouth felt so dry that I couldn't get the words out. Still, there was no other option and she was the perfect person to take advice from under the circumstances.

'Sanjana, what I'm going to tell you is very confidential. You better not tell anyone,' I made her swear. She nodded solemnly, 'You can trust me completely. But what is it about, why the secrecy? And do I have to keep this from Moh and Nandini too?' 'Especially from them,' I said fiercely.

Then I hesitatingly began telling her about Rohit, how I had felt attracted to him at first, our rendezvous in the park, the series of meetings after that and how I had fallen head over heels in love with him. Even before I finished, Sanjana, ever the dancer, her right eyebrow raised and her eyes prancing, interrupted, 'Ananya! So you too?! At least now you have joined the ranks of us mortals!' Then with a mischievous twinkle in her eyes, she said, 'No wonder you'd gotten so mad at me when I showed signs of interest in him, and I thought he was off-bounds because he was Moh's brother. I know better now!' With her eyes closed, face slightly upturned, she added, 'You are so lucky, Anu! I have only dated boys my age, but have always wanted to go out with an older one. Wish I could have had a boyfriend like Rohit—so sexy and so mature!'

Oh! Sanjana was getting distracted. And the thought of Rohit as her boyfriend annoyed me.

But right now, I had an important matter to deal with and the quicker I got to it, the better. So after chiding Sanjana, I plodded on. The fact that Sanjana had been there, done that, made it easier for me to tell her about my kiss, which she asked me to describe in detail. But I wasn't going to satisfy her morbid curiosity. I asked her the one question for which I had made the trip to her house. 'Sanjana, Rohit has asked me to come over to his house in the afternoon today. Should I go?' She looked at me as if I had gone mad, 'What kind of a question is this? You are asking me as if you have never been to Moh's house before!' Not meeting Sanjana's eyes, I said, 'It's not so simple Sanjana. Rohit has specifically said that no one will be home then. I know I love him, but I'm not sure if I should go. What do you say?'

As I said this, I felt foolish. I was sure that Sanjana would always know how to tackle such a situation. She had always been comfortable with boys. I wished I was like her—cool and sophisticated.

The pretty Sanjana, her eyes dancing in merriment, let out a whistle, 'So, it's like that, is it?!' I don't know what she meant by that, but I blushed. I think she noticed but thankfully decided not to torture me further. Then, on a slightly more serious note, she said, 'Anu, you go ahead and have a good time. Maybe he just wants to spend some quality time with you before leaving—watch a movie together or something. You can also take tips on cracking the entrance exams from him.' I wanted her to go on and cover the broad dos and don'ts, but just then her phone rang and the moment passed. Sanjana cooed in her honeyed voice, 'Hi baby, I'm busy now, call me later!'

Then she teased me, 'Remember the time when we had the sleepover at Moh's place. Moh had a fight with Rohit about something. Do you remember what it was about?' I cast my mind back to that night more than six months ago. Moh had burned a hole in each of Rohit's clothes to make him quit smoking, I remembered. We both laughed as we were reminded of the incident and I felt my tension easing a little and I felt better. Finally Sanjana asked, 'So has he quit or does he still smoke?' I told her that I had never seen him smoke, which I thought went in his favour.

I looked at the time. Time with Sanjana had flown. I had to go home, get ready and rush to be in time at Rohit's place. As I waved at her, she smiled slyly and shouted, 'Now just remember to be a good girl. And Anu! Whatever happens, *don't go all the way.*'

I nodded coyly at Sanjana and left.

Back in the comfort of my room, after a quick shower I lay down spread-eagled on my bed letting the air from the fan dry me, allowing me a few minutes to myself.

Book #2

Down came the rain and washed the spider out

13

For some reason, I was feeling very nervous, so I decided to wear my armour—my favourite sports clothes. I put on my blue T-shirt and white shorts. People have comfort food, I have comfort clothes. I combed my hair, pulling it in a high ponytail and securing it with a purple scrunchie, the colour of potassium permanganate. I slipped my feet into a pair of purple canvas shoes that I had recently bought.

Meeting Sanjana had definitely helped me clear my mind. Even though the visit wasn't necessary, it had calmed me down. I knew that I completely trusted Rohit and with that thought, I reached his house.

With my heart thumping like a steam engine, I rang the bell.

He opened the door and I almost swooned at the sight of him and his musky smell. He had a day's stubble, which only made him look even more... sexy! He was dressed in a sky blue T-shirt and white tennis shorts, the same colour combination as my clothes. He looked at me and grinned, 'It seems we are well matched in every way!' I gave him a small smile and looked down at my shoes, suddenly feeling shy and very unsure. As I stood rooted to the doorstep, I felt him hold my hand, 'Come inside.' I entered the living room and sat down on the sofa. I crossed my legs and for good measure folded my hands in my lap. What was the matter with me? Why was I behaving like some silly ten-year-old girl, rather than as a grown up?

Rohit didn't sit down; he paced the length of the hall. Suddenly he stopped, turned towards me and his expression unfathomable said, 'Anu, you know I'm leaving in two days.' I nodded, not trusting myself to speak. I was only too aware of the date. 'These last couple of months have been the best in my life and as you know somewhere along the way, I have fallen in love with you. I didn't want to, but it just happened. That's the reason I called you over today, to share this with you.' I sat spellbound, not able to believe what I had heard. Could it be true? Or was he making fun of me? But he looked serious enough, *and* he was Moh's brother; he wouldn't lie to me about something so huge.

A tiny proton of happiness collided with another and released a spray of happy protons which further collided with each other setting off a chain reaction which filled my entire being with delirious joy in a matter of nanoseconds.

He continued, 'I will finish my Masters this year and then will pursue a PhD. Though I will be coming down to India every six months for two to three weeks each time, I will find it difficult to cope with this separation. If I could help it, I wouldn't go at all. But I can't let my parents down.' I nodded my head vigorously at this, as this was something I could understand and relate to. 'As soon as I finish my PhD, I will take up a job in the US. It will only be a matter of time before you also graduate from IIT and then you could come to the

US for a job or do your post graduation. And we could be together then.' As he was saying this, I was drowning in his eyes and trying to absorb the intensity of his feelings towards me. Though I was not quite sure about the US bit, I was really humbled and touched by him making future plans for us together. I had never felt so cherished and special in my life before. I had no words to express my feelings; I blinked back my tears.

Rohit got up to get two glasses and a bottle of a golden liquid, which turned out to be champagne. 'No thanks, Rohit, not for me. I don't drink. Can I have some water instead?' Suddenly my throat felt parched and my voice, thick.

'Come on Anu, this is probably the last time we'll be alone like this before I leave, let us celebrate.' I found that my eyes were moist and knew that however uncertain our futures were, we had this moment with us for sure.

He pulled away and looked so lovingly at me that I didn't have the heart to say no and didn't need further coaxing. He poured me some champagne, and told me how to roll it around my tongue to enjoy it. I found the sensation quite pleasant and took another deep sip.

He was sitting next to me with his thigh pressed against mine. I felt heat waves flowing from his body to mine. He had already pulled out the scrunchie from my ponytail and was stroking my hair and neck. I felt every nerve end in my body come alive and pulsate. I kept my glass—which was empty now—down carefully and turned towards him. Leaning in towards him I whispered hoarsely, 'Rohit, have I ever told you how hot you are? I like it when your hair is ruffled like this.' Saying that, I tangled my fingers in his hair and ruffled it. I saw Rohit's eyes darken. I pulled him closer and softly grazed his lips against mine. I felt his sharp intake of breath as he murmured, 'Anu, you know what you are doing, right?'

Did I know? Deep in a corner of my mind, Sanjana's voice cried a warning that maybe this was going much too far and that it should stop. But before my thoughts could get coherent, I saw a malicious Aditi's face sneering down at me and saying, 'Boys don't make passes at girls who wear glasses!' I got the answer to Rohit's question. Oh yes, I knew very much what I was doing! I was in love and I didn't want this to end.

Suddenly, the kiss grew more passionate and demanding. I didn't even realize when we got up and walked towards his room, hand in hand.

He made me lie down on his bed and pulled off my shoes and started massaging my toes. The pressure of his thumb felt so good on my feet. I shut my eyes. He removed my specs and suddenly, I felt my T-shirt being tugged over my head. I realized that Rohit was lying down beside me. I looked down, terribly conscious, and crossed my arms over my chest. Rohit moved my arms away gently. I felt his hands all over me, caressing my breasts, moving down and massaging away the knots in my stomach, his fingers going round my navel. I forced my eyes open and saw Rohit above me, shirtless and saying, 'You look so beautiful, wearing only your chain and pendant, I can look at you like this forever.'

Then I felt a shaft of pain shoot through my body. The shock crystallized my thoughts for a fraction of a second. As I looked at Rohit, he said, 'Stay calm, Ananya.'

14

I was agitated and apprehensive about what had happened. The line I had no intention of crossing, had been crossed. I suddenly felt panicky and sought comfort from Rohit whom I trusted with my life.

'Rohit, what happened between us right now...,' I was not sure of how to handle this or even what to say.

'Chill Ananya, just relax. We did nothing wrong. You know I love you. I will get you some orange juice, it will make you feel better. I will just be back.'

As I sipped the chilled juice, the enormity of what had happened hit me hard. I felt confused, morose and depressed. And not to mention a bit dizzy and light-headed. However, Rohit was right. After having the juice and washing my face with cold water, I did feel better. I combed my hair and almost felt normal again. With Rohit, I was safe. As I stepped out of his room, I froze in my tracks.

Moh had just entered the house and saw me coming out of Rohit's room. She was back early. Luckily Rohit was comfortably lounging in the hall watching football. When he saw Moh, he said breezily, 'Hi Moh, how was the function?'

Moh looked at me and then back at Rohit, 'It was very

nice, though a tad lengthy. Mom and Dad will be back in an hour. Anu! What are you doing here?'

'She had come to meet you but since you were not here, I said she could play games on my laptop. Since you've come now, my babysitting duty is over. I'm going out now.' Though the part about him babysitting me rang shrilly in my ears, I was so grateful to Rohit for the lie. Behind Moh's back, Rohit smiled at me and was gone.

Somehow, Moh didn't look too pleased to see me. Her sullenness combined with my own guilt led to an uncomfortable half an hour between us when we half-heartedly played chess. Soon, Moh had checkmated me and after the game, I made an excuse, not meeting her eye, and quickly turned and fled.

When I reached home, I parked my cycle and walked to the hall with heavy steps. When I reached the door, I stood for a while, appreciating for the first time the effort that Mom had put in to do up the house and to keep it so beautiful. I don't know why, but for some reason, today I just stood there taking in the details. The hall had been done up tastefully, there was a beautiful Persian carpet in red in the centre of the hall and paintings by various artists adorned the walls. I noticed the rich silk cushions, vases full of fresh flowers and the sparkling chandelier. I gulped down a sudden lump that rose in my throat, crossed the hall and went upstairs.

Mummy and Papa were waiting for me, all dressed up. Their faces lit up as they saw me. Mummy said, 'Anu, you really look quite the street urchin. Quick! Wash up and come with us, we're going out for dinner.'

Babysitting duties, street urchin—today indeed was my day for getting compliments.

Mom liked me to be well-dressed and presentable—clean, well-scrubbed, wearing nicely washed and ironed clothes at all times—something that I took great pleasure in rebelling against. But today was an exception, I felt like conforming and not rebelling. I put on my best salwar suit in red and white printed silk and went out.

As I got into bed that night, I thought that only two days were left for Rohit to leave India. I suddenly felt a deep pain in the pit of my stomach. I also could not brush away the intense discomfort about what had happened. It was so not meant to be that way. However, I tried to comfort myself thinking about how much I loved him and about how even his future plans had included me.

He didn't call me the next day. I felt helpless and distressed as I could do little about it. I tried to immerse myself in my studies to keep from thinking too much about Rohit. There was enough of Gollum's stuff to keep me busy, but still my thoughts were on one track. Finally, on the eve of his departure, I couldn't stop myself. When I saw that Mom was comfortably settled in her chair and watching her favourite business channel on television, I dialled his number. I was suddenly butterfingered; the mobile threatened to slip out of my fingers. There was no response. I tried again and he picked it up on the seventh ring—yes, I was counting.

'Hi Rohit!'

'Umm, hi! Will you hold just a sec…yeah, tell me, Anu. What's up?'

He sounded a bit preoccupied, so I asked hesitantly, 'Are you busy? Should I call you later?'

'No, it's okay. Shoot.'

'Rohit, I really want to meet you at least once more before you leave.'

'Oh Anu! I'm dying to meet you too but you know how it is. I have packing to finish and say last-minute goodbyes to my friends. It seems difficult.'

He must have guessed my mental state in my silence as he said in a softer tone, 'You know baby I love you more than anything or anyone in the world. We will stay in constant touch, I promise. I'll mail you every day. And I'm carrying a very beautiful picture of you with me, so that I can look at it whenever I miss you.'

'Rohit, you have a picture of me? How come? Did Moh give you one?' I dreaded Rohit having seen one of our class photos in which I looked totally nerdy. I would have given anything to have snatched it back from him.

'No silly, I took a picture of you when you were lying down on my bed. You looked like a little angel, with your eyes softly shut and your hair fanning out on the pillow. I just had to capture you like that!'

'Oh no! Rohit!'

Suddenly I wished that he had my class photo instead. 'Please don't show that picture to anyone!'

'Of course not silly, it is for my eyes only. I love you Ananya. Do you love me?'

Me and my silly doubts, I thought.

'Yes, I do. More than my life.' With a promise to stay in touch and tears threatening to choke my voice, I put the phone down. Then I went to my room for a good cry, as it was beginning to sink in that I would not see Rohit for another six months and I wasn't sure how I would live through that.

Sanjana cornered me in school the next day during lunch break and eyes dancing with mischief asked, 'So ma'am, how did it go?'

I suddenly found her nosey, interfering attitude very irritating. 'It was as you said. We just watched a movie,' I said, keeping it short and curt.

15

After Rohit left, I went back to my studies with a vengeance. Though many times I caught myself thinking about him and his smile, with great difficulty I would drag my thoughts away from him. We wrote to each other, every day in the beginning. Then the frequency dropped, as he got busy with his paper submissions. On a whim, I wrote a long e-mail to Rohit that day, telling him how much I loved him and how I was already counting the days left for his return.

But even with such distractions, though pleasant, I was quite happy with the pace of my revisions. Within a fortnight, I had made up for lost time and was soon practising mock tests and question papers from previous years and scoring satisfactorily. I was confident of maintaining my lead position.

It struck me in the evening that my periods were two weeks overdue. Stressed due to dealing with my separation from Rohit and catching up with my studies, I had totally overlooked this fact. I was puzzled. Usually, my cycle was very regular. I thought of checking with Ma, but then decided to wait for another couple of days.

One more week passed and I was beginning to get worried. I went to look for Mummy but Amma said that she had gone to the temple. I went on the internet thinking that I would google it.

I searched for 'delayed periods'. The internet connection was particularly slow that day I thought, as I drummed my fingers on the desk. Finally, my wait was over and the screen came up. I opened the first link, then the second and the third. There was no doubt—the information was very categorical. Oh God! This couldn't be true. It was just one lone incident, for God's sake! Was this even possible?

Though we had both promised not to call each other due to the cost of international calls, and instead chat, or e-mail each other, I needed to break my end of the promise that day. I saw the time and quickly calculated that it would be early morning in the US. I dialled Rohit's number, but there was no response. I tried again but still nothing.

I sat with my head in my hands. What if I really was pregnant? What would I do? As I sat there in front of the computer trying to digest the information, panic engulfed me and a deep sense of regret as well. What a fine mess I had landed myself in! What if it was really true? What would happen to me, my life? What would happen to my dreams? What would I tell Mummy and Papa, and how would I ever face them?

I didn't want to be pregnant and I definitely didn't want the baby. My life would be over even before it started. How irresponsible had I been! Sanjana had rightly warned me, but I had also trusted Rohit. I tried his number again, but got no response. I desperately wanted to talk to somebody; somebody who would tell me that my fears were misplaced; somebody who would tell me what to do, but I couldn't think of anyone. Oh, the shame of it!

I had seen home pregnancy test kits mentioned on the internet. But from where could I get one? I surely couldn't buy one from the neighbourhood medical shop. We had known the owner for ages. I decided to take an auto rickshaw halfway across town. As I got down, I didn't take off the scarf that I had used to cover my hair and face with. At the medical store, I realized to my horror that I couldn't do it. I almost went back, but then I stopped. I fished for a piece of paper in my bag; my hands were trembling. With my hands shaking uncontrollably, I wrote down the brand name I had made a mental note of from the internet and handed it over to the chemist. As he read it, he leered at me, looking me up and down, trying to see my face and guess my age, as if he knew exactly what had happened. I felt as if I was standing naked and could feel tears stinging my eyes.

When the kit was given to me, I picked it up, paid for it, and fled. On the way, I tried reading the instructions, but due to the print being too fine and the auto shaking too much, I found that difficult. Upon reaching home, I ran straight to my room and opened the kit. Amongst other things, it said: For best results, take the test in the morning. I hid the kit in my cupboard under a pile of clothes.

I had no idea of what I chewed during dinner. I moved the food around the plate and when asked about what was worrying me, I mumbled something about being stressed because of my exams. I told Mom that I would take the plate to my room and eat there while studying. Mom looked a bit worried, but nodded. Once in the safety of my room, I flushed my entire dinner down the toilet. I had no appetite. Even the smell of food was making me nauseous.

I went to bed feeling ill. I prayed fervently for any disease, any calamity, other than this pregnancy. How I hated the whole thing. I spent the entire night—which proved to be the longest night of my life—tossing and turning.

I was up early the next morning when it was still dark outside. I took the test and prayed for the colour of the lines on the strip to stay as they were. But they did not. The test was positive. I felt my entire world come crashing down around me. I sat clutching the strip in my hand. Then I ran downstairs to call Rohit before anyone in the house woke up. It would be night in the US. I dialled a couple of times but still had no luck.

I got ready and went to school. Somehow, I found the strength to carry on with my routine mechanically, but remained lost and absent-minded the whole day. Moh looked very concerned when she saw my pale face and asked me what the matter was. I told her it was nothing and that I was just feeling a bit under the weather. Maybe it was a bug or something.

As soon as I reached home after school, I tried calling Rohit again, not caring about the time in the US. But again, no response.

I went to my room and sat on my bed, totally dejected. I was at a loss about what to do. I pulled up my knees, laced my arms around them and my head dropped yielding in to the gravity of depression. Why was Rohit not picking up his phone? There was no doubt that he would support me, but first it was important to reach him on the phone. I didn't want to do this through e-mail.

I sat there for a long time. Fortunately, no one came to my

room, as they must have assumed I was studying as I usually did. Slowly, the brightness of the sky outside got bleaker and soon it was splashed with streaks of orange, pink and purple.

As I sat contemplating my fate, images kept flashing through my mind as in a turning kaleidoscope. One sees through a peephole and sees one picture. Then one turns it and the colourful glass pieces rearrange themselves to show a completely different picture. I briefly wondered if the world was like that. Nothing was fixed, nothing predetermined— everything fluid and subject to change. There were decisions to be made at every point and this was a continuous function, not just a one-step process. Infinitesimally small changes in decisions could change the future just as a slight flick of a finger, lighter than the touch of air, could change the picture in a kaleidoscope.

I saw a grown up version of myself wearing a helmet and supervising the construction of a bridge. The thought that this might never happen now wrenched like a knife in my stomach. Contrasting this image was one of me walking down the school corridor with a bloated stomach. I heard sniggers and then, 'Oh, she's an easy one. If I knew this about her, I would have had a go at her myself.'

I couldn't bear it any more. My own mind was set to torture me. I cried. In the twelve hours since I had discovered that I was pregnant, this was the first time that I had cried. And once I started, I couldn't stop; I didn't even try to. Unchecked, the tears flowed freely down my cheeks.

Much later, totally exhausted both physically and mentally, I opened my laptop and surfed the internet aimlessly to divert my mind. Though I had no intention of knowing about the happy lives of my other friends, the parties they were attending, the movies they were watching—I found myself logging on to Facebook.

There was nothing to hold my interest there except some extremely irritating updates, game scores and horoscope predictions. I was just about to log out when a chat window popped up with a hi. It was from Rohit. I felt as if my prayers had been answered.

'Hi,' I replied.

'Missing you Anu. How are you?'

'Not fine at all. Have been trying to reach you. Can you please call me ASAP? Urgent.'

'My number has changed, am calling you right back.'

Within seconds I saw a US number flashing on my mobile. Rohit really was so considerate; I knew I was saved now. He would help me out of this mess somehow. With a deep sigh releasing my pent-up tension, I picked up the phone.

'Hi sweetie, what is it? Stuck with some problems that need help or missing me?' Rohit sounded just the same as always—teasing, mischievous and so loving.

'Rohit, I'm pregnant,' I blurted out not able to indulge in any niceties.

'Anu, have you lost your mind? It is not possible! We did it only once! Are you sure of what you are saying? Do you even know what this means?' It must have been my imagination but I noticed that a shrill note had crept into Rohit's voice. It was not possible. Rohit who had always been so caring, so loving and who had pampered me so much. Anyway, I was too far gone to dwell upon it.

'It is true Rohit. I have missed my periods. I have taken pregnancy tests, not once but twice, and both times they have come positive.'

'Rohit, I love you. I love you more than life itself. I dreamed of spending my entire life with you. But what do I do now? I'm stuck so badly,' I couldn't help a note of panic seeping into my voice. I think the desperation and the hopelessness in my voice finally reached out to him.

'Anu, look, I love you too. I'm sorry, though there is no excuse for this; I guess I just got carried away. But you don't worry. We will work something out. I'm with you. Listen, I have to go now. Someone's at the door. See a doctor discreetly if you can. I will stay in touch.'

And Rohit's voice cut off from the phone even though I wanted to hold on to it just for a moment longer. Though I felt a bit assured after having a chat with him as he was on my side and said he loved me, I was still as unsure about my course of action as I had been before.

I carried on like a mechanical robot trying to keep a tight rein on my volatile emotions. I felt like crying most of the time and to cover up for that, I tried forced laughter. But even that effort would leave me exhausted, unable to do much else. Each passing day worried me more and more. All I was receiving from Rohit were some bland assurances—about how things would work out, how they would be okay once again, I had no idea. I wanted to go to a doctor but how would I even find one? I kept pushing the thought away, thinking I would go the next day, but just couldn't muster up the energy or the courage.

Days were spent trying to keep up the charade and when I fell exhausted into bed at night, sleep would prove elusive. The smell and sight of food made me nauseous and I would leave most of it untouched. The only saving grace was that Mom and Pa were very busy at work and were coming late, so I was saved the effort of offering them any tiresome explanations.

16

I glanced at my answer sheet in mute horror. It was full of red correction marks and, not only that, I had also flunked the test. It was not uncommon in the coaching class for students to flunk the tests as Gollum made sure they were incredibly tough, but it had never happened to me before. I sat there feeling sick, my hand covering my mouth, praying desperately that the tears that had welled up in my eyes would not roll down. It would be the height of embarrassment; I contained them with a supreme will of effort.

Still, a lone tear escaped its confines and rolled down my cheek. Surreptitiously, I pulled out a tissue and wiped it away and slipped out of class without taking sir's permission. Back home on my bed, I kept looking at the answer sheet. It was totally crumpled by now.

I got up in the morning to find myself still clutching the answer sheet. I felt terrible, as if my guts were churning. I ran straight to the bathroom on wobbly legs; I had a terrible urge to throw up. I bent over the sink and retched and retched, but nothing came out. I was bathed in perspiration from the effort. I collapsed on the bathroom floor, the tiles feeling cold under me. After a while, I got up and dragged myself to bed.

I heard a knock on the door. Amma walked in with the usual glass of milk. Just the sight of the milk made me want to throw up again. I shouted, 'Amma take the milk and go away, I don't want to see you!' She stood stuck to the ground, shocked at my unreasonable outburst and a look of deep hurt crossed her face. I knew that I had crossed my limits. Amma had been a stand-in mom for me on so many occasions and she surely didn't deserve this. I pulled myself from the brink of insanity that I seemed to be plunging into, to apologize to her, 'I'm sorry Amma. I'm not feeling well. Thoda juice la sakti ho kya?'

I felt marginally better after having the glass of juice and got up to get ready for school. Somehow, I must have lost weight as my skirt felt loose. There were dark circles under my eyes, something I had never noticed before. I looked what I was—sick. However, appearances were the least of my concern now. Who was there to admire me anyway?

At school I was able to make the dash to the girls' toilet in the nick of time and saved myself from disgracing myself. I threw up in the toilet and flushed it away. It had been too close. I was very short with everyone at school, especially Moh. Suddenly, I wanted no one around me, no friends, no parents. When I reached home, I was so exhausted that I collapsed on the bed without even taking my uniform off.

I must have dozed off for when I opened my eyes, it was dark outside. Shoot! I had missed my coaching class. While earlier the thought of bunking a class was mortifying, now it provided a welcome relief. I was not able to take in anything that was going around me and I didn't have the strength to look at another answer sheet covered in red.

Over the next couple of days, my efforts were entirely focused on making it to the bathroom on time. I was throwing up every few hours. 'How long will this go on?' I thought miserably.

'Rohit, I'm feeling exceedingly sick. I'm throwing up every few hours. Nobody knows but it is only a matter of time before someone guesses. Amma has been giving me strange looks. I have even stopped going to my coaching classes. Tell me what to do. Please come back, at least for a few days. I'm feeling very lonely.' I shot the mail off praying for a quick reply.

My phone rang. I let it, it was an unknown number. It rang again. I ignored it. When it rang the third time, I finally picked it up. Might be something important.

'Ananya Sharma?' it was Gollum. He had never called before nor was he known to do such things.

'Yes sir,' I replied weakly, sure that I was in for a big scolding for having bunked the classes.

'Where are you and why are you not coming to the classes?' he continued in his trademark firm and severe tone.

'Sorry sir, I had a stomach infection. I will come next week.' Though what dramatic change would happen next week, I had no idea.

'And I thought it was because of your poor performance in the last test.'

Sir was very astute and clearly able to see through my excuse. It was half the reason anyway.

'Ananya, don't be put down by such small things. You are a very intelligent child and have great potential. This is a very critical time; the exams are just months away. If you encounter such blips, don't be discouraged, instead redouble your efforts. I have great expectations from you,' his severe and gruff voice was tinged with a note of concern and warmth, a trait I had never suspected in him. Somehow, realizing that he'd shown too much of his good side, he said sternly, 'I want to see you in the class soon.'

'Yes sir.'

The line was cut off without any acknowledgement from his side, no polite bye.

I went to the coaching class the next week. However, I was not able to focus on anything as I was feeling very tired and nauseous. As I reached home, I ran to the bathroom and emptied the contents of my lunch. Exhausted, I collapsed on the bed. Amma came twice to call me for dinner I think, but I just waved her away.

I felt someone shaking me. I opened my eyes blearily to see Mom's outline against the dim night light. 'Anu, are you okay? You look quite ill. Amma is telling me that you have not been eating well these last few days. I'm sorry but I have been coming so late that I didn't get a chance to talk to you.'

Mom helped me get up and fluffed the pillows behind me to make me comfortable. What is it about moms that in spite of having a thousand issues with them, one instance of tender, loving care makes your issues dissolve like salt in water. I felt perilously close to tears. I had a surge of desire to confide everything in her. She would put everything right.

'Mom, I think I may just have caught the bug that's going around the school. Plus, I think the stress of long hours of school and then coaching classes has been pulling me down a bit.'

'Anu, take it a bit easy. I know how desperately you want to get into the IITs, but don't burn yourself out like this. Maybe you need a small break.'

'Amma, Anu is up now. Can you get the soup here only?' Mom called out. 'Anu, I think you should see a doctor, I can go late to office tomorrow.'

Though I had been contemplating going to a doctor, the thought of going to one with Mom panicked me. This was something I just couldn't do. 'No Mom, I'm feeling better now. We don't need to see a doctor.'

'Okay. We will give it another day and then we will see. Amma, just put the tray down here and wet a napkin and get it.' Mom wiped my forehead, which was damp with perspiration with a cold wet towel and started feeding me the soup. I felt much better than I had in a long time and could share a smile with her. However, I was starting to feel sleepy again and once the soup was over I said, 'Mom, bas aur kuch nahin. I want to sleep.' I saw Mom look a little worried, but she covered it up with a smile and said, 'Okay, Beta. You sleep now. But be there for breakfast on time, Amma is missing your appetite. Goodnight.'

In the morning I dabbed a bit of compact on my face to conceal my paleness and put on a bit of Vaseline on my chapped lips. I looked slightly healthier with all this. I was able to return Mom's smile when I went down. 'You are looking slightly better Anu. Take proper rest till you get okay, otherwise you will only make yourself worse.'

I pushed my breakfast around my plate. I just couldn't bring myself to eat anything. Aware that Mom's eyes were on me I got up suddenly and said, 'Amma please pack this for me.

I will eat it at school. I'm getting late.' I couldn't keep up the charade of being healthy and happy in front of Mom for too long and it was better to leave before the cracks showed.

In the lunch break, I had just come back to my desk after making the by-now-routine dash to the toilet. I put my head down on the desk to rest for a while. I suddenly felt a tap on my shoulder; I looked up to see the three angels, my very dear friends, whom I'd been cold-shouldering these last few days, standing in a semi-circle around me. Moh was the first to speak, 'Hey Anu, are you okay? What is the matter? You are not your normal self. And you are looking quite ill also.'

'You know you can tell us anything,' Sanjana said.

'Come on, Ananya. Don't be like this. If we have done something because of which you are not talking to us, do tell us. We won't mind. We all have been missing you so much,' Nandini was chewing on her bottom lip, looking very unhappy.

'Not only us, even your fans are missing you. I can't tell you the number of guys who have been asking me what is the matter with you,' this salvo was from Sanjana. 'What?' I was immediately worried, had everyone, including the boys noticed my condition. It was possible that Sanjana was making it all up; she was quite capable of doing it. Anyway the boys would use any excuse to get to talk to her.

I told them that it had absolutely nothing to do with them, but I avoided looking at Moh as I said this and told them the by-now practised lie of not feeling well. 'You have been working too hard. You need to have some fun in your life; let us all go for a movie tomorrow. What say?' There were nods of approval from everyone at Sanjana's suggestion and I found myself saying yes too. It was impossible to not be infected by her enthusiasm.

I was dimly aware that the passing days didn't improve my situation. Something had to be done and that too urgently. I was not able to chart any course of action. I had to contact Rohit urgently, but how? He was not responding to my mails and was not seen on chat either. Maybe I could try calling him in the night.

I kicked off my shoes as soon as I reached home and threw my socks on top of them, not in the usual neat manner; my feet were killing me. I dragged myself up the stairs and collapsed on my table.

There was an e-mail from Rohit. This is what I had been waiting for—maybe there had been a genuine reason for the delay. My heartbeat picked up as I opened it; herein lay the key to the end of my misery.

> *Hey Ananya!*
>
> *I'm sorry I couldn't write to you earlier because I have been very busy with my thesis. As your good friend, I'm very sad to know that you have not been keeping well. May I suggest that you see a doctor and follow their advice? Hope the preparations for your exams are going on well. I will be coming to India in couple of months' time, maybe in Dec and look forward to meeting you then.*
>
> *Yours, Rohit*

What bullshit?! My entire being screamed. Busy…good friends…coming in Dec…what was going on? Rohit had written as if we had shared nothing ever but a cup of coffee… as if I had nothing more than a common cold. My entire life was at stake and he was busy with his thesis, would come in

December! I would be four-five months pregnant by then! Things were just not adding up. Even though I was the one saddled with the mess, it was his fault too! He was responsible for all this. None of this would have happened if he hadn't plied me with champagne that day. Unused to alcohol in any form, my control had slowly slipped away. Bit by bit, the scales fell from my eyes. Rohit didn't love me.

He never had, he had only pretended to. It was all one-sided. He had cheated me and used me. Oh! What a fool I had been. What a first-class one!

I felt a tide of anger surging within me, replacing all other feelings. Then another tide building on the first one, then another…

I picked up the glass of water next to me and threw it at the opposite wall. It shattered into tiny pieces.

The sound further fuelled my fury. I tried to control the shaking of my hands… One by one each and every book from the book shelf was torn and flung across the room. After decimating my entire treasure and not being able to look at what I had done, I dashed back to my table to write one final e-mail.

'Rohit, you have put me in the most impossible situation and instead of standing by me, you are washing your hands off this. I just don't know what to do, please understand that I cannot ask anyone else for help. This is not America. My life is totally messed up—I feel like there is no point in living anymore! If you have even one bit of decency left, come down immediately and help me get out of this mess.'

Sending the mail felt cathartic. I looked around the room; my once neat and beautiful room was a mess. I closed my eyes to it. One more thing to explain to Amma. Just then my phone rang; it was Rohit. Maybe I had been too harsh in judging him. It could be that he had changed his mind and was flying down to meet me. I felt my anger evaporating and a tiny hope rising. I wiped my tears and reached for my phone…

I could barely recognize his voice—he sounded shrieky, high-pitched in fury, or was there a note of fear? I shivered despite the physical distance between us.

'Don't take the moral high ground with me,' he said. 'You were equally responsible. Don't tell me you didn't know what we were going to do when we were alone.'

'I didn't, Rohit, you have to believe me,' I said.

'Well, what's done is done. We made a mistake, but there's only one way forward and I can't do anything from here. You'll have to go to a doctor and get an abortion done.'

'No, I can't do it alone!'

'Listen, don't be stupid. It's no big deal. I cannot come down now. You'll ruin your life and mine too.'

'I'm ruined anyway,' I said. 'Rohit, I trusted you and you took advantage. You are responsible for this. I will tell everyone. You called me over, you took off…'

'Don't threaten me, Ananya. It won't work. I have a picture of you sleeping in my room without a stitch of clothing on,' he cut in.

I stood benumbed. I sobbed into the phone, 'No, Rohit— you would never do that. Please help me, you said you loved me.'

'No, Ananya, I never loved you,' said the remorseless, unfamiliar voice. 'I was attracted to you, but that's all. And it was an interesting challenge—to get under the skin of the Ms

Studious. What we had, what we did was just two people getting physical. I thought you knew the game—your friends like Aditi surely did—how was I to know you would take it so seriously?'

I knew by now that Rohit didn't love me; I had figured it out myself. But to hear him say it after his numerous proclamations of love earlier just killed me. It really did.

The voice droned on, but my ears could not hear any more. My shaking hands did not have the strength to hold the phone any more, which fell to the floor spilling out its guts—the back cover, the battery and the SIM card.

I felt sick, sick to the core of my being. I put on my sneakers and went out. My legs based on some prior muscle memory took me to the park. The park, which held so many beautiful but now painful memories for me. To banish those memories and to punish myself I jogged. I jogged and jogged and jogged—jogged against a mounting hysteria; jogged against increasing nausea; jogged against a rising discomfort in my stomach…

I just have a vague recollection of how I managed school the next day. I tried my best to put up with Sanjana's teasing remarks as she insinuated that the only matter with me was that I was lovesick and was missing Rohit terribly. Her comments made me feel even more acidic and after a short walk with her, I went back to the classroom. I tried my best to be attentive in class. But I knew it was a façade, nothing of what happened around me really registered. Even my grades were in a free fall. I had not only lost my lead, but was way behind most of the class.

It was late afternoon when I sat cross-legged on the bed by

now used to the presence of my tears. I let them run their full course in the privacy of my room after having made a superhuman effort of keeping them at bay all day long in public. I contemplated the options in front of me—Tell Moh? Tell Mummy? Somehow contact a doctor and get an abortion done—was it safe, did doctors even do it, would it mean hospitalization—how would I keep it a secret then? I had reached a dead end. I felt panicky and overwhelmed and cupped my face in my hands.

And then, as the dam of emotions burst open through my tears, I slowly felt a change coming over me. I made up my mind. However difficult and traumatic it was going to be, I had to confide in Mom. I couldn't handle this by myself anymore now that Rohit's desertion was complete. However, when, how and what to tell her?

Finally, as the last orange streak in the sky turned an inky blue, I went out to look for Mom. But she wasn't back yet. I called up her up, and she said, 'How are you feeling Anu? I was just going to call you.'

'I'm fine Mom. When will you be back? I want to have dinner with you today.'

'Sweetheart, I would love nothing more than that. But I need to make some presentations for the upcoming board meeting. However, I will make it up to you. What about dinner at your favourite Italian restaurant on Saturday?'

A large portion of my life was made of Mom saying '…will make it up to you. What about a dinner or movie over the weekend?' I thought one more of this, one more of being the second priority in their lives, wouldn't hurt. But somehow it did.

'Okay, Mom.' It could wait another few days till she was free.

'Hey, are you okay?' Mom sounded a trifle concerned, a bit sad and very tired.

'Yes, Mom, see you.' By now one more lie didn't matter.

'Amma, I will have dinner in my room,' I told her as I carried my plate upstairs because I couldn't stand her scrutiny further and also because I wasn't hungry. She had given me vague looks since finding my room in a mess yesterday but thankfully had not questioned me or told Mom anything.

I flushed down the dinner. The empty bookshelf in my room haunted me; I switched off the light and went to sleep.

I don't know what woke me up. Was it a bad dream or some pain? I got up from the bed but my legs seemed shaky as if unable to support me.

And then, I felt a sharp pain in my belly. It was nothing like what I had experienced before, and much worse than the cramps I suffered during my periods or occasionally, while playing. The pain kept returning in waves. I clutched my stomach and rolled into a foetal position and lay like that on the floor. After a while, I felt something wet between my legs... I saw it was blood. My mind in a haze, I screamed for Ma, but wasn't sure if it was in my mind or aloud. And then, waves of darkness mercifully engulfed me.

17

When I opened my eyes, I was on a stretcher, being wheeled inside a hospital. I saw a white-faced frantic-looking Ma walking beside my stretcher. Tubes were glued to my arms and I faintly heard Ma say, 'Anu, what happened? Tell us.' I opened my mouth but no words came out so I looked away from her. I suddenly felt very drowsy and soon felt myself slip into blissful oblivion yet again.

I don't know for how long I had slept, but I was starting to hear faint voices. I heard unfamiliar voices say,

'...another case of a teenage miscarriage.'

'The girls these days are so shameless. They have no morals... just run after the boys.'

'Look at the trauma they cause their parents. Her mother has not stopped crying from the time she arrived at the hospital and her father is not able to look anybody in the eye. He kept looking away when the doctor explained what had happened, as if it was not his daughter but someone else.'

I cringed with shame and a different kind of pain enveloped me. The voices moved away after a while and I slipped into unconsciousness again, with no desire to ever come out of it.

I'm drowning. I can't breathe. As panic engulfs me, I feel a set of strong arms pull me out of the merciless waters. As I try to blink the water out of my eyes, I'm so comforted to see Papa smiling down at me. I'm four years old and Papa is trying to teach me how to swim. Once again, he holds his hand flat under my belly to support me as I try flapping my arms and kicking my legs. As we near the other end of the pool, he lets go suddenly and shouts encouragingly, 'Swim! Reach the end of the pool!' I'm sick with fear but even at that age, too proud to give up. I keep up with my flapping and kicking and finally I find the edge. Somehow, I manage to cover that distance all by myself. I turn to look at Papa and see the most heart-warming smile on his face; his arms stretched out towards me and saying, 'Now swim back towards me.' This is the beginning of my love affair with swimming.

Then the kaleidoscope turns.

I'm in Class V and as usual, seated on the last bench in class as I'm the tallest girl or rather, the tallest student in my class. I'm fighting with Amit for having kept his pencil on my side of the desk. We had used the pointed end of a geometrical compass tip to draw a line dividing the desk in two, the borders of our domains inviolable. But Amit's only mission in life seemed to be to drive me to the point of extreme irritability by continuously pushing his things into my domain.

Then suddenly I hear the class teacher calling for me. I freeze, fearing she will put me down in front of the whole class for causing a disturbance. However, something is not right. Her tone is almost soft, not scolding. And wonder of wonders! She is not angry, but says that I have topped the class. I can't believe my ears! I mean I have never even been in the top five before, there must be some mistake, but she is holding my report card high in the air. As I take it from her and walk back, I smile and my heart thumps in rhythm with the sound of applause.

The whole hall has burst into a deafening applause—the students, teachers and judges are on their feet clapping. Sanjana and I have just finished delivering a charmingly convincing performance of Othello and Desdemona. Our names have been announced for the first prize in the fancy dress competition and, even though I'm very excited about it, there is a niggling pang of discontent as well. I would always be Othello, looking ugly, with my face painted black. I would never be the beautiful, petite Desdemona. Now in Class VII, I have started becoming aware that my tall, lanky and bony frame is not something that favours anyone's attention.

I'm now arching my back while in mid-air over a pole and jumping over the raised bar that many have been unsuccessful at. I'm winning the gold in the high jump category. I'm running fast and taking off in the air, managing a bronze in the long jump event; the principal proclaiming me as the school topper. Images of Papa's promotion and the party at home flash in my head. Fighting layers of my sub-consciousness, I'm trying to think how I have come to be where I'm right now. I, who was the brightest kid around town and I, who had never harmed anyone.

As I returned to the present, a quiet sadness spread over my being and crushed me. It was as if my mind had exhausted its quota of pleasant memories.

I saw a small child in a white Grecian gown walk towards me. The child was a little far and I could not see its face clearly. With my arms extended, I ran towards it. But the fog thickened and suddenly I couldn't see anything. I was shouting, 'Come back, come back!' but no one answered. And then I saw Rohit's face floating above the mist, twisted with malice. He laughed cruelly at me and the sound of his mean laughter kept getting louder. I screamed and ran, but not fast enough, as if my feet were being weighed down by lead.

The fog bleared my vision and I hazily realized that the ground beneath me was getting even wetter. All of a sudden the mist lifted. I saw, to my horror that I was in a swamp; its foul smell enveloped me. As I turned to retrace my steps, I found my feet stuck in the mud. Try as I would, I could not get out of it. As I thrashed about madly, I kept sinking deeper and deeper. The quicksand felt like a living creature that was sucking me down into its bottomless pit. I felt suffocated and started screaming for help. Then I felt two arms pinning me down, pushing me further into the quicksand. I struggled harder.

Then, through the fog, I heard Mom saying, 'Anu, wake up, wake up. You are having a bad dream.' As the layers of unconsciousness peeled away, I saw the child again, but this time in a black dress with a hood and an accusing finger pointed at me.

As I came to, I saw Mom peering down anxiously at me. However, this was something I could not share with anyone. I was drenched in sweat even though the room was cold. I held my hand to my throat, which felt parched and was hurting as if someone had run sandpaper on its inside. I closed my eyes. Mom sponged my head and face with a cold towel. After a while, I opened my eyes and saw my pain reflected in hers. Then I hugged her and cried for what seemed an eternity. Ma said in a whisper, a whisper that wrapped layers of deep anguish in it, 'Anu, how did this happen? Did someone force you? Who was it? I cannot believe it.'

'I'm sorry Mom. I'm very, very sorry. I wanted to tell you about it, but somehow couldn't. But Mom right now I cannot talk, please give me some time.'

She held a glass of cold orange juice to my lips and I sipped it thankfully, 'Okay Anu, but at some point of time you will have to tell us the entire truth. You father is most upset.'

'Did she say anything? Who was it?'

The thing I'd dreaded the most, happened in the evening—Pa came to visit me. He hesitatingly asked Ma these questions. The fall from grace of his darling daughter, the one he doted on and who he always took pride in showing off to the world, was so steep that he probably couldn't orient himself. 'You know Sudha I can't believe what has happened. Our Ananya? She always stood taller than others; she was the class prefect, a topper! Where did we go wrong Sudha?'

He continued, 'We must not let word get out. We must speak to the doctor and ensure absolute secrecy and confidentiality in this matter. What will happen to her future? It would be disastrous for both her as well as us. I'm so ashamed. I don't know how I will face anyone if word gets out. Meanwhile you try and find out who it was. Then we will see what is to be done.'

I kept my eyes shut; it was easier to continue pretending to be asleep. However, I felt a touch on my hand and slowly opened my eyes. Papa had come to sit next to my bed—my father, who had so much faith in me and who loved me unconditionally. His head was bent. He looked tired and beaten. His face was unshaven and his white shirt, crumpled. A tear rolled past my closed eyes. 'Papa,' I said softly. As he looked up, I was shocked; it seemed as if the light had gone from his eyes.

Papa wiped my tears with his hand but then he stood up and left the room without saying a word and that hurt me more than any remonstration would have.

18

It was, I think, my third or fourth day in the hospital. To their credit, my parents hadn't asked me any questions till now. But now, stroking my hair, Mom cautiously asked, 'Beta, we need to know what happened. We didn't press earlier as you were very ill.'

It was the toughest thing ever to tell Mom about Rohit and what happened. But at least I owed them the truth. She had the right to know. But how could I share the story of my shame with the one person I always looked up to and script her shame and her fall as well? However, selfishly so, I wanted to share my pain with someone. It was threatening to stifle me and tear me apart.

With my head bowed, slowly I told her the humiliating tale. As I finished and looked up, I realized that my pain had only heightened. Like an alien in a Star Trek episode, it had mutated, multiplied and was causing even more devastation. And now, it was in Mummy's eyes and mind, probably taking an even bigger shape than in its creator's. Mummy whispered, 'Rohit, Moh's brother? How can it be?' Absentmindedly, Mummy was stroking my hair. Immensely tired and soothed by her action, I dozed off.

'...I'm not going to leave him... will kill him with my bare hands... is a crime... I will speak to our lawyer... I will file a police complaint... that boy will spend the next ten years in jail...' Papa was pacing up and down, looking murderous. And for the first time in my life I was afraid, really afraid.

Seeing me awake, Mom got me some orange juice. After I finished it, Papa came and sat near me. I had never noticed a vein in his forehead before; it was throbbing madly now, 'Beta, I need to go to Moh's house and talk to her parents. We just can't let things be the way they are. You... we... we all have suffered too much. They can't be let off the hook just like that. They need to be told and some action needs to be taken... against Rohit.' Though he had kept his voice low, I knew he was furious.

I was shocked. I had never heard him speak like this before. Summoning my remaining reserves of strength I screamed, 'No, Papa!' Then, lowering the tone of my voice, I begged him. 'It was not their fault,' I whispered. I wanted to shackle the alien bent upon destruction; it couldn't be given new innocent victims to feed upon.

But Papa barely heard me. He continued, his voice a strange mix of anguish and anger as he said, 'Can any suffering be greater than a father's to see his child in such a state? We have suffered and I will make sure that they suffer too. I'm not going to leave any of them.'

I couldn't believe that this person was my father. Forget harming anyone, Papa had never even wished ill for anyone! And now he wanted revenge? Papa wanted revenge! Pa, who followed a high code of personal ethics. And then I understood. He was grieving for his child that was lost to him, lost to him forever. Only then did I get a sense of the magnitude of the pain that made him so weak.

But I had to stop him, not only for the sake of my best friend and her family but also for his own. Because I knew that if he did what he said he would, he'd never be able to forgive himself later.

I beseeched, 'Papa, please don't do this, I beg you. Cross your heart and swear by me that you won't do this.'

Papa looked at me for a while and then finally said, a certain weight pressing his whole being down, 'No, Ananya. I will soon talk to his parents.' Saying this, Papa left the room.

After examining me in the evening, the doctor said, 'She is fine now. We can discharge her tomorrow.'

I had mixed feelings about going home. Though being in the hospital was very depressing, especially being subject to the nurses' censorious stares, I still felt protected and cocooned from the real world.

I couldn't meet Amma's eyes when I entered the house. I don't think anyone had told her, but she knew. I realized that she had always known it, probably even before I did. She knew my cycle even better than Mom did and the associated symptoms—the acne, the fatigue, the cramps and my tantrums. She would give me a paste of chandan and haldi for my acne, methi seeds soaked in water and crushed for my cramps and would sit oiling my hair with a special herbal oil she prepared for me at home. The oil's recipe was like a witch's brew—it had coconut oil boiled with hibiscus and curry leaves—and according to Amma, it had trusted soothing properties. It suddenly dawned upon me—we had not indulged in this ritual for over two months now. Of course she knew!

I knew my moment of truth with Amma would come sooner or later, but for the time being I was grateful to her for letting me avoid her.

On the way back home, there was complete silence in the car—not the sort of post-dinner comfortable silence but an eerie one. It was loaded with despair as if you were trapped inside a glass room and you could see the person outside screaming, but you watched in helpless fascination as no sound filtered through. Everyone in the car was screaming, I saw that from my glass room—Papa was shouting infinite pain, shame and revenge and Mom was shouting sadness and guilt. I saw them screaming and when the sound of the silence grew too loud, I collapsed inside my glass room with my hands covering my ears.

I trudged up the stairs to go to my room. I saw my phone on my table. There were a few missed calls, most of them from Moh. I ripped out the SIM card and threw the phone in the dustbin; there was no one in the whole world I wanted to speak to ever again. The action sapped whatever energy I had left and I flopped down on the bed exhausted.

I had no appetite and over the next couple of days—I kind of lived in a haze weaving in and out of consciousness. I have no idea how many days passed liked that.

I woke up and was relieved to be in my room—safe from damp evil-smelling swamps—but I felt the emptiness within me. I touched my stomach and thought of the little life that had pulsated there just for a little while. I recognized the swamp for what it was—the guilt of murder, the loss of a precious life. Though I felt cold, I was drenched in sweat. I picked up the napkin and mopped my brow. I felt incredibly thirsty and reached out for the glass. It was empty… I checked for the jug… somehow it was empty too.

I shivered a bit as I pushed aside the quilt and swung my legs down. Never fleshy, now my legs looked like two long bean boles. I pulled on my robe and picked up the jug. As I crossed my parents' room, I heard a strange muffled sound coming from within as the door was half open. Maybe it was not so late. I moved closer to the room and stood hesitatingly just outside the door. And then I realized what it was. Mom was sobbing, and her sobs had a very primal tone to them. In between her sobs, certain words floated to me, 'I failed Anu as a Mom… she deserved more, much more.' Hearing her sob like this, in the dark, under the quilt, something tore in my heart. I knew I would carry the sound of Mummy's voice, the pain and the hopelessness in it, to my grave. I would never be able to forgive myself.

Oh, that alien was wreaking havoc within me, breaking my heart into a million pieces. When it attached itself to Mom, it did something more sinister—not only did it break her heart, but it also brought to the surface a feeling of guilt at having somehow failed me. It would never let her be at peace now. And in Papa the alien had mutated even more. So much so that he was completely transformed and ready to throw away a lifetime's worth of virtues, values and beliefs.

19

I knew I had to start going to school sometime or the other, though I had no idea how I would cope. I had no clue what Mom and Pa had told the school and the coaching classes. I shuddered suddenly at the thought of Gollum's ire. How would I face it? At home Pa and Ma were behaving in an artificial manner, going about their tasks normally and behaving as if nothing had happened. But it all looked forced. Sometimes I wished that instead of acting as if nothing had happened, they would air the issue, talk to me about it. Maybe even scold me, shout at me, whatever. Anything but carrying on with this nerve-grating charade of normalcy. But then again, I wished that they wouldn't do that. I couldn't face them. Not yet anyway. Maybe it really was better this way. Maybe in the act of pretending, trying to forget, we could convince ourselves that it had never happened. I busied myself with the task at hand, trying not to think—because in whichever direction my thoughts turned, they only brought pain. Faces of my friends from my past life glided in front of my eyes, only to fade away. And Rohit? Full stop. Dreams of cracking the IIT exams and becoming a successful civil engineer? Gone forever.

I was so lost in pretending, forgetting, not thinking, that I failed to see the emotions that simmered just under the surface. The charade of normalcy was just that—a charade. Nothing was forgotten, nothing was forgiven.

I had just finished the glass of orange juice which Amma had left for me when I heard the sound of raised voices coming from the hall below.

As a slow recognition of the voices dawned upon me, dread spread around my chest slowly tightening its grip. I wanted to run away from the source of the commotion, but instead found myself creeping towards it.

Papa was saying, his voice raised high, 'It is only because of Rohit that Ananya is in this state today. Ananya, who was a model child, who everyone tried to emulate but did not even come close.'

I peeped in through the curtains and saw Uncle and Aunty sitting on one sofa and Pa and Mom on the sofa opposite them. I felt enveloped by the waves of shame that rose and swirled around me at the topic of this discussion, at the centre of which was I. What would Pa have told them, what would Uncle, Aunty have thought of me? Did Moh know too? Why was Pa doing this?

'He led Ananya astray, cheated her, betrayed her! And look at the relationship that was there between the two of them. He was my daughter's best friend's brother! We know how attached Anu is to Mohini and we always trusted your family. We never questioned the time Anu spent at your place, though in hindsight it feels that we should have.'

I felt tears sting my eyes and the memory of the hours I had spent playing chess with Uncle rose to the surface of my mind. Moh was so like him—always calm, always gentle.

Pa continued, 'What kind of upbringing have you given your son? Does he have no shame, no morals, no sense of responsibility? He has squashed the life out of our Anu, she has lost her childhood forever, she can never walk with her head held high. I have checked on Rohit—it seems Ananya was not the only one. Your son is quite infamous or shall I say famous for "certain" things.'

Did Pa realize that with each word he was killing my soul bit by bit? Did I want to hear the sordid story of my affair once again? But of course, he did not know that I was there. I looked at Mom; she was sitting with her eyes downcast.

Suddenly, Aunty retaliated, 'Bas bhaisahab, bahut ho gaya! We are also feeling sad about the incident. Just because we are sorry, does not mean that you can say whatever you want to! You are talking about the upbringing we have given Rohit. What about the upbringing you have given Ananya? Maybe if you had cared for her enough she would not have spent so much time at our place and gone around seeking attention from others. Maaf kijeye bhaisahab, I'm also fond of Ananya and respect you all, but I must say that she always lacked care at your house.'

She continued, 'Taali kabhi ek haath se nahin bajti. I have spoken to Rohit. He is feeling bad at what has happened, but he said that Ananya led him on. He has sent me the e-mails that Ananya wrote to him. From that, it does not seem like Ananya is some innocent, naïve girl!'

Usually soft-spoken, Aunty sounded waspish today. Does protecting one's own bring out the worst in everyone?

'Vandana, stop it. Don't do this. They are already suffering, don't add to their pain,' Uncle said softly but firmly to Aunty.

At least he was on my side. I couldn't make out what Aunty was doing, but it could not have been good. I felt betrayed by her. From where I was standing behind the curtains, the sofa on which Uncle and Aunty were sitting was on my right and the one on which Mom and Dad were sitting, on the left. I was somewhere in the middle. Mom had not spoken a word, but was sitting with her head tipped down. I saw there was some kind of movement on the right sofa followed by the sound of papers shuffling.

'Things have gone too far to stop. For once, I'm not going to listen to you,' continued Aunty.

'Dekhiye bhaisahab, you see for yourself. See the mails that Ananya wrote to Rohit.'

Oh no! Anything but this. At that moment I wanted to evaporate into the ether. I saw Pa give the papers a glance and pass them on to Mom. I knew that he was shattered, shattered into a million pieces. The entire fight left his system then and he looked beaten. Mom looked up from the papers in her hand and said softly, 'What has happened cannot be undone. It is true that despite whoever was at fault, it is she who has borne the brunt of their actions and suffered miserably. May I request you to leave now?'

I shut the curtains and ran towards my room. Blindly, unseeingly. I crashed into a solid wall. It was Amma. There was no room for pretences any more, I was too tired anyway. I turned into her warm bosom and cried. She held my hand and led me to my room. Once in my room, she made me lie down and stroked my hair. Neither Mom nor Pa came to my room; they were probably still trying to come to terms with my complicity in the matter.

I had lost track of the passage of time. I could divide the day into morning, afternoon, evening and night by the movement of the sun. Sometime the next day, Amma ushered Moh into my room.

Her face looked lifeless. I had never seen Moh looking like this before. As she looked at me, I saw deep pools of pain in her eyes. A thought crossed my mind that possibly, if there was someone suffering as much as me, it was Moh. 'Anu, I'm sorry, so sorry. You have been my best friend forever and I love you. But I love Rohit too. I see you suffering and my heart breaks, but Rohit is suffering too. Pa called him yesterday and told him that he was no longer his son; so ashamed was he of him. How I wish none of this had happened!' Then as if sensing what was going to happen, she fell silent. Moh was my soul sister. We had grown up together and were totally attuned to each other's moods. However, what cut me now was that she was not able to see her brother's treachery in this. I was hurt that she even had a choice to make and had not trusted me implicitly and completely.

My survival instinct kicked in and I felt it was time to sever this bond both for my own good and hers. It was a relief to know that she had applied for a transfer to another school; Uncle and Aunty understood that it would not be possible for us to keep seeing each other.

After Moh left, I heard a faint sound of laughter. I saw two little girls with their hair in two plaits, not more than five or six years old and as scruffy as street urchins playing hopscotch and cackling away merrily to their hearts' content.

As I looked harder, the scene changed. The girls were a little older now, around seven or eight, but as scruffy as the younger ones. It was summer. The girls were sitting under a mango tree laden with fruit. They were kneading the mud with water and, with the resultant dough had made mud furniture—sofas, beds and chairs. As they set their 'designer' furniture to dry in the sun, they ground one red brick into powder and used the powder to colour and decorate it. Pleased with the results of their hard work, they set out to collect the fallen ripe mangoes and without washing them, sucked the sweet fruit.

The two merged into 10-year-olds, their hair styled in short bobs now, challenging the boys to a fight with water bottles. The boys, to their credit rose to the occasion, but were no match for them. The two were caught in the frenzy of winning the fight when their teacher walked into the classroom. Caught and pulled out of the class by their ears, they were both dragged to the principal's office. Apologies followed, but they could not prevent the strict notes of admonition sent to their parents.

Was I seeing the same set of girls? They seemed to grow up very fast. The scenes kept changing even faster. The girls were shooting up like weeds in a garden—they played badminton together, swam together and of course studied together.

The girls were Moh and me.

Then I saw one of them holding the other's hand under water. I almost pulled my hand back as I remembered the pain arising from the burn. This was Diwali, we were both dressed in outfits that we hated but even this attire could not kill our spirit. In the foolhardiest of manner, we were taking turns burning crackers in our hands, lighting them from diyas directly and flinging them away. Our fun lasted till I got a second late in throwing the cracker away and it burst in my hand. Oh God! How my hand had burned. The question of running to our parents for help did not arise, lest we got the scolding of our lives! After a few minutes of keeping the hand under water, when the burning sensation became tolerable, Moh applied Burnol. While she took care of it, she kept talking to me about irrelevant things to distract me from the pain.

But now Moh, my Moh, even she could not help soothe the burns on my soul. I would probably forget Rohit with time, but I was sure I would never ever forget Moh. I would miss her so much.

20

'Anu, it is almost three weeks since you last went to school. We have been getting calls from your school as well as coaching classes. We have told them you were down with a severe case of chickenpox and your Papa has managed to get a certificate from a doctor to show that. Beta, we cannot hold it longer. I know it is not going to be easy for you, but you have got to make the effort. For your own sake. Maybe seeing your friends again would make you feel better.' This was the first acknowledgement between us of the 'incident' since I had come home. My only conversation these days was with Mom; Pa had been totally avoiding me since Rohit's parents came home. I was not stepping out much from my room and even my meals were brought up and from my window I could see Pa's car leaving early and returning late. It seemed he was finding a way of release from his pain by immersing himself in his work. Maybe it would work with me too if I went back to my studies.

I had been thinking about going back to school too. Maybe that's what I needed, the distraction of friends and diversion of studies to keep my other thoughts and nightmares at bay.

'Alright Mom, I will go from tomorrow onwards.'

My reflection in the mirror looked like a vision of a B-grade horror movie actor crossed with a circus clown. The dark circles under my eyes which even my specs couldn't hide and my cheekbones jutting out provided the scary aspect and I seemed to be dressed in a uniform at least two sizes too big which looked comical. I adjusted the school belt and tightened it around my waist.

Pa said he'd drop me to school every day while going to the office and would send the car and the driver to pick me up later. As we drove to school, I felt extremely anxious. I started thinking how my friends would react after not having met me for the past few weeks. What did they know? What would they think and what would I tell them? How could I face them after what had happened and how was I going to deal with curious glances and either inevitable sympathy or censor from them? Would they judge me? How would I ever answer their questions—I was barely managing to keep myself in one piece and even the smallest little thing could lead to a collapse.

As Papa dropped me at the school gate, I turned to him and said, 'Papa please take me back home. I can't go through this.' He held both my hands and said, 'None of your friends know anything about what happened. The hospital has kept everything confidential and when your friends called, your mother told them you were down with chickenpox.'

With a heart full of trepidation and on shaky legs, I left for school. As I entered the building and walked slowly to my classroom, I saw that nothing had changed. There were still students hanging around in groups talking and laughing, dispersing hurriedly before the bell rang for the assembly, teachers were moving towards the staff room to deposit theirs bags before they attacked the students, the peon was as usual slumped in one corner. Nothing had changed and yet everything had. Yesterday I was an insider, a cog in the whole system, and today I was the outsider.

I saw curious glances thrown my way as I walked to my class. When I entered the classroom suddenly there was a hushed silence. Everyone stopped talking for a second and stared at me. It must have been my altered appearance. No beauty queen in any case, now I positively looked like a scarecrow. I said a weak hi to some of my friends and moved to my desk. Amit was already there but he didn't meet my eyes. And once again I felt a twinge of regret at losing his friendship. I had suffered huge losses because of Rohit and had lost two of my best friends—Moh and Amit—as well. I wondered what else this phase would claim.

Luckily the bell for the assembly rang just then. I walked slowly out of the room, much like an old person. The spring in my step was long gone. Luckily, none of the teachers mentioned my absence or my 'illness' and the day progressed smoothly enough and it was lunchtime soon. At lunch break Sanjana and Nandini breezed into my room, anxiety written all over their faces. They came and hugged me. It felt good to see them, a bit therapeutic. I was wrong to keep away from them for so long. Now I had only these two friends left. As usual they had carried their snack boxes with them and while we shared the food, they filled me up on the latest in the school. However, I got the impression that they were making deliberate and conscious attempts at keeping the conversation light. Even their smiles seemed a bit forced. Maybe it was just my imagination. My friends were incapable of any subterfuge. If there was anything, it would come up soon enough. But most of all, I missed Moh's company at lunch time.

Over the next few days, I noticed a change in my classmates and somehow I had a niggling feeling that it was not related to my altered appearance as I had thought earlier. Outside the group of three divas who were my best friends, I had few friends. So wrapped up was I in my group, and so complete within it, that I had never bothered about making any more friends. The only exception had been Amit. Now my earlier lack of tact and subsequent lack of friendships came to haunt me. For some unknown reason, many of my classmates were now avoiding me, not even bothering to respond to my greeting. I shivered as if a spider had suddenly run down my spine.

I felt hushed whispers all around me, eyes that avoided making contact, classmates who avoided me as if I were the plague, and some stares grew bolder. It seemed that the teachers had changed too—some became softer towards me and some harsher. I wondered if it was all real, or was I getting paranoid. Was it possible that I was losing it? I withdrew further into my shell lest someone discover my paranoia, and would just step out of it for a brief while during the lunch break when Sanjana and Nandini continued putting a falsely cheerful charade. The classes continued at their normal pace and I made peace with my steadily declining marks in all the assignments. Amit was topping everything, but didn't seem happy doing so. Things were so topsy-turvy now that they stopped making any sense.

Sometimes I desperately wished that I could talk to some friend. But whom? Sanjana? Nandini? What had happened was huge and throbbed wildly inside me, threatening to rip me apart as it wanted to come out. But I could not let it come out, however much I wished. I could share my pain, my misery, my shame with no one.

In my coaching classes I saw a kindness in Gollum's eyes which I had never seen before and except for the appearance of big red marks and comments scribbled all along the margins of my worksheets, he didn't say anything. And for this I was infinitely grateful.

And then it happened—when I was the least prepared for it.

I had started putting in a bit of effort in my studies and this was starting to reflect in my assignments. My grades slowly began to improve. Today when my answer sheets for the math quiz were handed out, a small smile appeared on my face, probably for the first time in months. I had got an A+. On a reflex I turned towards Amit to show him my marks, but stopped in time. I think he noticed the small movement but chose to ignore it. I couldn't wait for the lunch break to show this to Sanjana and Nandini. I knew they would be happy for me.

Today we had to meet in Nandini's classroom. I picked up my lunchbox in one hand and my answer sheet in the other and suddenly I found a spring in my step.

Hushed whispers. Only they were louder this time.

'So what do you think about her?'

'She is really cool man, despite what has happened she still behaves like a queen bee. Or maybe it is because of what happened.' Guffaws and laughter. The whispers grew louder and walked ten paces behind me. So they knew, they all knew. That's why they had been avoiding me.

'She has an attitude for sure, but she is really not my type. I don't like sticks, they poke. I like curves.' Loud laughter, I walked faster along the corridor. I was sweating, I wanted to reach Nandini's classroom quickly.

'Oh, I don't mind. I wish I knew she was easy! I too would have tried!'

Suddenly, there was a thud behind me followed by a yowl. I turned on a reflex to see Karan—one of the rowdiest and the most notorious boys of our class who barely managed to scrape through—holding his jaw with one hand and his eyes popping out.

I stood rooted to the spot shaking from top to bottom wanting to run away, but not being able to.

'Hey, chill, Amit. Why pick a fight over a girl? Anyway, didn't she choose that chikna from the US over you?' Samar, Karan's partner in crime said.

However, he too was silenced when Amit's fist made contact with his jaw. 'Karan, Samar, I'm warning both of you. One more word from you guys and you have had it.'

'Hey Amit, don't think we don't know what you are trying to do. You are trying to impress her so that you too can get some favours. We have no problems with that, let us all share,' Karan said with a leer.

A small crowd was beginning to form attracted by all the commotion. I was mortified. Amit's face was distorted with rage, he drew his fists again and was about to throw a punch when he was pulled back and restrained by his friends Kabir, Dhruv and Dev. Amit strained against them, but the three of them held him tight, not letting him go. The whole crowd had split in two groups—one supporting Amit and the other Karan and Samar.

'Amit, tujhse toh school ke baad nipat lenge,' Samar said. I could not stand there any longer; I turned around and ran to Nandini's classroom, sobbing.

'Yes Ananya, everyone knows. Abha's uncle works in the same hospital where you were admitted. I think he was discussing your case with Abha's parents when she overheard. I remember you mentioning that she wanted to be friends with you earlier but you ignored her and didn't accept her friend request on Facebook too. I know she's weird. Maybe she thought that this was a perfect opportunity for revenge and for garnering some attention for herself too. She spread the word around. Nandini and I had a huge fight with her when we came to know, but by then the damage was done,' Sanjana ended in an anguished voice.

My answer sheet slipped from my fingers and fell to the ground. My snack box followed and its contents spilled all over the mark sheet. I sat with my head clutched between my hands.

'What should I do? Sanjana, Nandini tell me, what *should* I do?'

'Anu, none of it is your fault. Don't let some losers break your spirit. Walk back to your class with your head held high and show them the stuff you are made of. Anu, we are and always will be with you,' Nandini said with wisdom which I had previously never seen in her.

I somehow managed to walk back to my classroom. However, I was not able to hold my head high and slinked into my seat. I looked at Amit, his face looked like it was carved out of stone. The rage was gone, replaced by sadness. As I sat next to him, he said, 'Ananya, I'm really sorry for what

Shilpa Gupta

happened.' Was he referring to what happened today or what happened with Rohit? Maybe both.

'Let me know if I can help in any manner. You can always count on me.' Amit's voice was as kind and gentle as if he was speaking to a child. I felt tears of gratitude sting my eyes and I nodded a weak yes to him. Having Amit back as a friend was a blessing, which I had not counted on and was the sliver of silver lining in this otherwise dark day. However, I had made up my mind that I was not going to attend school from tomorrow onwards.

Just then the bell rang, signalling the end of our lunch break. It had not even finished pealing, when the peon appeared in our classroom. We all hated him. He was lazy, untidy and always chewing paan, the spit of which dribbled from the corner of his mouth. He always adopted an irritating, supercilious way towards the students or maybe it was a façade to hide his deficiencies. Why would our principal even put up with such a chap?

Wiping the spit with his handkerchief, which was stained red, he called out, 'Amit Nagarajan, principal saab has called you to his office. Come right away.' Having issued the summons he walked off.

While I was worried, Amit looked calm.

Amit came back in the middle of the period looking grave and I was not able to talk to him till the end of the period.

'Amit, what happened?'

'Nothing.'

'You have to tell me.'

'Well, Karan and Samar complained to the principal that I had hit them both. They had got their friends along who were witnesses. Sir asked me if it was true and I said yes. I told them that they were harassing a girl student and this could be checked with Kabir, Dev and Dhruv. However, on repeated questioning also I refused to divulge your name, as I didn't want you to be dragged through it. Anyway, on acts of indiscipline Karan, Samar and I have been suspended for a week.'

Amit. Suspended. This was not possible. Just last year he had been awarded the All-Rounder trophy. Amit was also the class prefect. Class prefects were looked up to, they were not suspended.

'I'm sorry Amit. It was all because of me. You should not have interfered.'

'I'm not sorry. Listen Ananya, there was no way I could have stood by and let anyone talk like this about you. We have been friends and that means something to me. If I have managed to shut those two guys up and the rest of them as well, the suspension would only be a small price to pay.'

That night, my nightmare recurred. Rohit was joined by Karan, Samar and whole lot of other guys whose features were indistinguishable. They were closing in on me—leering, menacing and laughing—as I sank lower and lower. I screamed and screamed.

'Anu, wake up. Wake up! What happened? Sip some water.' Mom was holding me and rocking me. My bedside lamp was on.

'Mom, I'm not going to school from tomorrow. They know, Mom. Everyone in the school knows,' these were the last words I said before I lost consciousness.

21

The blackness enveloping me became greyer and slowly turned white as I surfaced out of the quagmire. I saw Papa standing at the window, holding the grill, shoulders slumped and head tipped down. Slowly, he raised his head, let go of the grill and stared at the rising sun. Then, as if deriving his strength from that perpetual source of energy, he squared his shoulders and turned around. This was the first time since I had come back from the hospital, which was maybe six weeks ago, that Pa had come to my room. During this time only Mom and Amma had been coming to my room. Only now I realized how much I had missed having him around. I was shattered at the change in his appearance—his jet-black hair was peppered with grey and there were fine lines around his eyes. He had lost weight too—his clothes hung off him. It was only now that I understood how much I had hurt him. And he probably had been avoiding me all this while not only as a way to cope but also to spare me the knowledge of the pain he had undergone.

There was no escape for me now. I saw a shattered soul in front of me, a broken man—only a vision of his earlier self. When Pa saw that I was awake, he started saying something but seemed lost for words. Where there was a huge comfort earlier between us, now there was awkwardness. I couldn't meet his eyes and looked away. Earlier I was happy, proud and carefree, but today I was only ashamed of my actions. More than at any other time, I now wished that I could go back to the time when I was his darling daughter, the one he wholeheartedly doted on.

'Anu,' he called out my name. As I looked up, I saw him put on a cheerful smile which, if anything, caused more pain and embarrassment for me. 'Good morning. How are you feeling?'

'Better, Papa.'

'Mom says that you don't want to continue going to school. Is that true Beta?'

'Yes, Pa. I tried but I'm not able to cope either in school or in the coaching classes.'

'Listen, Beta, what I would suggest is that you skip school for a few days. Anyway your Diwali break is coming up. Let us see how you feel about going back after your break. Right now you focus on taking some rest and getting well.'

Just then Mom walked in with my breakfast tray. Papa nodded at her and left the room.

Sanjana and Nandini visited me every day and their visits were something I really looked forward to.

I heard a bomb going off in a distance. Diwali was quite a noisy affair in our neighbourhood and the celebrations began early. It was my most favourite festival. I would always participate in it with gusto and we would all try to outdo each other with the brilliance, noise and the sheer number of crackers each one had. I loved everything about Diwali—the loud and noisy crackers, the sweets, decorations and exchange of gifts. Everything. This was a time of the year when I even indulged in some girly things like the making of the rangoli in front of my house. In fact, I was quite good at it and my rangolis had their own share of admirers amongst my friends and some of Mom's friends too. I lit the diyas in neat rows all around the house and wore a silk salwar kameez. Diwali was indeed a gala affair in our house.

All this was in my past life. However, this year I was not able to summon any enthusiasm for Diwali. From my window I saw rockets going off in a distance ending with a brilliant shower of multi-coloured stars in the sky. It was a very pretty sight. As if on cue Mom walked in, 'Anu Beta, Fatima Aunty is here to take your measurements for the salwar kameezes. Are you comfortable, shall I ask her to come up?'

'No, Mom, I just don't feel like celebrating Diwali this year. Please leave me alone. Send Aunty away.'

'Anu, listen. You cannot sit cooped up in your room all the time. You love Diwali. At least get the dresses done, then we will see.'

'Okay, Mom,' I said, giving in, not having the strength to fight any battles. Plus, maybe I owed it to them. Maybe Diwali celebrations, however superficial, would banish some of the gloom that hung around the house.

It was Dhanteras today, the first day of the Diwali festival. Amma made a small rangoli and lit diyas around the house. Mom asked me to get ready, as the visitors would start coming soon. I changed into one of the new salwar kameezes that Amma had put on the bed and came down after getting ready. However, there were no visitors. We kept waiting but still no one came. To hide her confusion and to bring some cheer, Mom suggested that we all go out shopping for some new vessels, as is the custom. We went to a jeweller's and Mom bought a set of six silver glasses and a tray. When we came back home, we saw lots of cars parked in front of our neighbour's house, indicating that their annual Diwali card party was on.

'Sudha, are we going for their card party?'

'We have not received the invite. Maybe they came to invite us while we were out.'

'Amma, did anyone come?' Mom asked in a false cheerful voice which failed to hide a note of desperation.

'Nahi Memsaab.'

No visitors. No invitations. Mom looked at Pa who went up without saying a word. The gift boxes that Mom had bought for distributing stood stacked in a corner and their sight depressed me further. I picked up the top one, flung it on the floor and went up to my room.

The next evening, on the day of chhoti Diwali, I refused to dress up once again, not even to please Mom. I sat in the hall in my faded jeans and an equally well-worn tee, flipping through a magazine half-heartedly when the doorbell rang. Mom's face lit up and that moment I pitied her. She had come to rely on such small things to find a meaning in life. Before she opened the door, she turned towards me and her eyes had a silent appeal. Sighing, I went up to change.

A cackling of sound poured in and life breezed into the hall. It was Sanjana, her elder sister, Sucheta Di, and her three kids—eldest son Ishaan and two newborn twin girls—and Uncle and Aunty. Ishaan ran forward and hugged me and my earlier black mood lifted a little. Di looked resplendent in a red silk saree. Motherhood really suited her. I pushed down the thoughts that were just beginning to surface. The sight of the newborn twins sent a sharp pang of guilt through me.

Greetings and gifts were exchanged and snacks served. Amma gladly offered to take care of the twins while everyone sat down to chat. Sanjana forced me to come out and along with Ishaan we burst a few crackers. Just then the gate opened and we saw Nandini walking in with her parents. I knew how happy this would make Mom; she was trying so hard to keep things from collapsing around us by hanging on to traditions and customs. Maybe we were going to have a normal Diwali after all.

Perhaps encouraged by the success of the previous evening, Mom came up with the suggestion of us visiting friends and relatives on the main day of Diwali.

'Sudha, are you sure this is a good idea? If the usual set of people have not visited us this year maybe it means something and we should take a hint from that.'

'There could be various reasons for their absence Kamal. But look at the difference Sanjana's, Nandini's and their families' visits have made to Anu. She looks much better today. I think it will be a good idea if she goes out and meets more people. It would do her good.'

They carried on this conversation as if I was not around. I kept looking down, pushing my kaanda-pohe around the plate. My opinion was not asked for, and was not offered. But I severely objected to Mom's idea.

The most well-intentioned plans have a habit of going horribly awry, at least in our case.

'Where first?'

'Mr Nagarajan's house? Amit is a good friend of Ananya's also.' Pa nodded.

Aunty was surprised to see us but she hid it well and was very courteous. While the grownups sat and chatted, I noted that the atmosphere was a little stiff and formal and not as relaxed as it used to be. However, Pa and Uncle soon got into an animated discussion regarding work and it made the atmosphere a bit more natural. Amit looked very nice in a white and red sherwani with a matching stole. While I was very self-conscious, he was totally at ease. He grinned and told me that though his parents were not at all happy about the suspension, he quite enjoyed it, as he hardly ever took leave from school.

'I really needed the break. What with the studies at school and Gollum also going into overdrive, I was totally losing it. One day I even bunked Gollum's class and played cricket with my friends. I cannot tell you how liberating it was.' Though I felt guilty and responsible for being the reason behind his suspension, it was a pleasure to see the old Amit with his mischievous smile and twinkling eyes.

However, the next instant he sobered down, 'Anu, I have not been going to school because I was suspended. Kabir told me that you too have not been going. You have stopped coming to Gollum's classes as well. Why Anu? You simply can't let guys like Karan and Samar get the better of you. They will think they have won. You have to fight back.'

I so didn't want to talk about myself, about school and what had happened that day at school. My voice cold, I said, 'Amit I'm not going back to school.' Amit sensed my withdrawal, but didn't back off, 'Anu, you have to come to school. I will come and drag you from your home if I need to.' I knew he meant well, but I was getting tired. I looked at Mom and managed to catch her eye. She read the plea in my eyes and inviting them to come to our house, she got up to leave.

The visit was not a disaster and even Pa looked a bit relaxed after having enjoyed a drink or two with Uncle and discussing work, which was his passion, his lifeline.

'Where to now?'

'Let's go to Kaamna's house. Normally they are always the first ones to visit us, let us visit them first this time.' Kaamna Aunty was Mom's colleague and like her had only one daughter—Vidhi, who was a couple of years younger than me. Kaamna Aunty would often send Vidhi over to our place to discuss her homework and school problems with me and whenever we met she would extol my virtues and give my example to Vidhi, much to my embarrassment. Vidhi was a nice girl, sweet but not very bright. Over the years, as I helped her out with her assignments, I had become quite fond of her as she was quite a pleasant girl. As our car turned the corner, I saw Vidhi dressed in a pretty green and red salwar kameez, going inside the house.

Kaamna Aunty seemed to lack her usual warmth. There was coldness in the air, which made me instantly uncomfortable. I looked at Mom, she seemed to be feeling the same thing and a look of uncertainty crossed her face. However, we couldn't just turn around and leave. Only Pa seemed unaffected. While the adults indulged in some polite conversation, I felt restless. 'Aunty, can I go to Vidhi's room?'

'Beta, she is not at home. She has gone to give sweets to our neighbours. She will probably be late coming back.'

My jaw dropped. I looked at Mom, she looked crestfallen too. Aunty was lying so blatantly and she knew that we probably guessed her lie, but didn't seem to care.

Mom recovered first. She looked pointedly at her watch and said in a tinny voice, 'Kamal, Savita Di is expecting us. We are already late, shall we go?' Lie for a lie. Both sides knew about it and made no effort to hide it. Suddenly, the whole atmosphere was poisonous. Pa looked perplexed, but didn't question Mom. I was hyperventilating and was out of the room even before Mom and Dad had finished saying bye. Was I some kind of contagious disease that Vidhi would contract?

Back in the car, Mom slumped in her seat. I was sitting diagonally across her in the car and saw her close her eyes and take in a few deep breaths. 'Kamal, let's go home. I think I have a headache coming on.'

'What happened Sudha? You look pale. Did Kaamna say something?' In a small voice Mom told him briefly what had happened. Pa cursed under his breath. Then after a while he said, 'I cannot believe how shallow people can be. They have always taken Ananya's help and now they have turned their back on her. I agree with you. We should probably go home. However, now that you have mentioned it I actually think we should go visit Savita Di. It has been long since we last met.' Savita Bua was Pa's cousin, and very fond of us.

Bua greeted us warmly and gave us sweets. That improved our mood a bit. Then she said, 'Ananya, Rupa and Sumit, why don't you all go inside?' Pa smiled at Mom and then at me to indicate that we had made the right choice in coming here. We were not treated like pariahs here.

We sat on the bed in Di's room and Sumit got a deck of cards. He dealt out the cards for a game of rummy. I was still feeling raw from the humiliation suffered at Kaamna Aunty's hands and was not able to pay any attention to the cards. I kept losing.

'I'm hungry,' Sumit said. 'Di, can you get me something to eat? There are so many goodies kept in the hall!' Though only a couple of years younger than me Sumit was really such a baby, mollycoddled by both his mother and sister.

'Okay, I will go. But don't cheat and look at my cards while I'm gone. Anu, keep an eye on him.'

'Di, you sit. I will get the snacks,' I volunteered as I was sitting at the edge of the bed, closer to the door.

'Kamal, how could you let this happen? And Sudha, I know you are a career-oriented working woman and all that, but how can you let your daughter run around unchecked? Don't the two of you have any sense of responsibility? And now after the incident, instead of hiding her away, you are flaunting her—sending her to school and visiting people! As if you are proud of what has happened? Arre kuch to sharam karo!'

'Didi, what are you saying? Just stop,' Pa had not raised his voice but I recognized his dangerous tone.

'Kamal, people do not like to hear the bitter truth. But the truth is that we had fixed a very nice match for Rupa. The boy was from a very well-to-do traditional family and their demands were also very reasonable. Your Jijaji had gone to their place last month and done the roka. We were planning a formal engagement sometime after Diwali and a wedding mid-next year.

'However, because of you all now all our dreams are

shattered. Somehow, they came to know about Ananya and said that they would not have a daughter-in-law from a family where the morals were so loose. Your Jijaji pleaded with them and told them that we were not very close to each other. Besides the entire community knew about the roka and if they rejected our daughter who else would marry her? He even offered to double the dowry amount, but they didn't relent. They have called off the marriage,' Bua burst into loud sobs.

'Kamal, you know that we have been grateful to you for helping us in our time of need when I needed a job. But this is too huge and we can't risk Rupa's marriage prospects further. I'm very sorry to have to say all this to you but my daughter's marriage and my family's happiness are at stake,' Phupaji said getting up and folding his hands indicating the matter was closed.

'Anu! Come let's go!' Papa thundered.

Even as I crossed the hall to follow Ma and Pa, I wished I could disappear. Was there no place left for me in the whole world? I felt sharp pricks of shame, humiliation and anger all over my body.

'You both sit in the car, I will join you in a while,' Pa said handing the car keys to Mom. He leaned against the window of the car and took out a cigarette. I saw his hands were shaking and it took him many attempts to light it. Pa, my iron man, was crumbling.

22

'Doctor, how long do we have to continue with this medication?' Pa asked in a voice laden with worry. 'It will surely have side effects, right?'

'It is important to keep her sedated for some more time. By then, hopefully her trauma will subside and maybe a natural shock absorption mechanism will kick in; it all depends on her state of mind and her willpower to get better.'

'And if things don't improve in few days? Then what will we do doctor? We cannot have her lying here like a vegetable!'

'She has been through a lot of trauma and maybe at a subconscious level, does not want to return to face the real world. Anyway, the Diwali outing was not a good idea, especially after what happened at her school. I cannot emphasize enough on the importance of ensuring that she suffers no additional stress for some time. Anything additional, however trivial, could just push her off the edge. As it is, we are dealing with a borderline case here.' The doctor's tone was censorious, which in a way pleased me. I hoped that now my parents would give me some attention. I was so tired of always wanting their attention; it had always gnawed at me just under the surface of my skin.

'We have to slowly work towards building a positive attitude in her and a will to live.'

I felt the stab of a needle in my arm and passed out.

'Anu! Sanjana, Sucheta and Nandini have come to meet you and they have got something for you.' I kept the book down and saw Sanjana and Nandini enter the room carrying a huge parcel and walking gingerly.

They laid the parcel on my bedside table and opened it.

There was a huge jumbo-sized chocolate cake inside it with 'HAPPY BIRTHDAY ANANYA!' written across it.

I raised my eyes at Mom. She nodded. How could I not even register today? My birthday was usually the most important day for me!

However, even as I turned eighteen and crossed a very important milestone, nothing enthused me. But I could not let my friends down and with fake enthusiasm I cut the cake. Even as I indulged in the ritual, I wondered silently that it must have been two weeks since Diwali! I had completely lost track of time.

I was being pressed down on the bed by strong arms. A needle was jammed into my arm.

'Sudha this is all your fault. All you have ever paid attention to is your career and totally neglected Anu.'

'You know very well that I took up my job to pay off the loans we had taken to marry off your sisters. You also cannot deny that the additional income has not been handy in the past. We would not have been able to afford many things, indulge in various luxuries on a single income.'

'Oh! Come on, Sudha! The indulgences, if anything, were for you. Who wanted foreign vacations every year? Who wanted to buy a bigger house? The plush interiors, a landscaped garden and servants on call, are all a part of the lifestyle you wanted, not I. All I ever wanted was a simple life. And please, I never bargained for my daughter being neglected.'

'It is fine for you to say all this now. When Ananya was born, I spent four years sitting at home twiddling my thumbs because I needed to take care of her. Where were you then? I will tell you—you were so busy climbing the corporate ladder that you were never around. My career suffered because of that break. I had to fight tooth and nail to regain my position.'

'You and your career. If you were not so bloody ambitious, and instead paid a wee bit of attention to what was happening at home, all this wouldn't have happened. At least I made some time for Anu but you were always so busy. But for your neglect, Anu would not have ended up like this.'

'So it is fine for you to be ambitious but not for me, Kamal? You and your double standards! I'm so tired of it all.'

Oh no! I didn't know there were so many fault lines running just under the smooth surface of our home. Had I been the earthquake, which turned these fault lines into cracks? I had no desire to return to this home where accusations were flying around, each meant to kill the other person bit by bit.

I was spaced out most of the time between the real world and my nightmares. However, I had not imagined the tension in Ma and Pa's relationship. It was for real. They barely spoke to each other anymore except to discuss me and only when it was absolutely unavoidable.

'Look Anu, look who has come to meet you! It's Sanjana and Nandini.' I heard Mom's voice faintly but was not able to respond. I willed myself to break the barrier of my mental exhaustion and get through, but the effort was too much.

'Anu, you must get up, your friends have come.' I felt something wet on my cheeks. I raised my hands to wipe it away.

'Aunty, don't cry. Look, she's just opened her eyes,' I heard Nandini say.

'I don't want to live. I want to kill myself,' I sobbed.

'Hush, what are you saying? See we are there for you, we love you,' Sanjana said in a kind but worried voice.

Even my parents no longer knew when I slept, when I was awake and when I was in the mid-zone between waking and sleeping. I kept my eyes closed and when I was sleeping my mind was awake and aware of things happening around me.

'The doctor says the medicines are no longer working. He suggests we could try therapy, as in go and meet a psychologist,' Pa's voice seemed weighed down by the burden his soul was carrying.

'You take the appointment, I will see to the rest,' Mummy said firmly.

I surprised Mom and myself by agreeing to see the therapist.

Book #3

Out came the sun and dried up all the rain

23

The next day Mom got me ready as the therapist was coming home to meet me. My reflection repulsed even me—it was like skin stretched tightly over my bones. I looked positively ugly. I had always been underweight and had lost another seven kilos in the past few months and according to the doctor, I was now nearly anorexic. I had never noticed the change in myself, but I saw now that I looked like a skeleton. There were dark circles under my eyes and my cheekbones and collarbones were jutting out.

Mom took me down to Pa's study. The therapist, a woman fortunately, was already there, waiting. After some small talk, she asked Mummy to leave.

'Hi Ananya, I'm Karuna. It's a pleasure to meet you,' she said,

Karuna, the compassionate, a part of my mind registered.

Her handshake was warm and firm, something that should have reassured me, but somehow didn't. At first, seeing Mummy leave, I panicked. But as I turned back to the therapist, something about her calm demeanour calmed me down too. Her voice was sweet and gentle, almost hypnotizing. She began by asking me about my school, parents and friends.

I started slowly, my vocal chords had not been used much the last few weeks, or maybe even months and my voice sounded rusty and raspy even to me. I cleared my throat and sipped a bit of water. I wiped my clammy palms on my jeans. Haltingly I told her about my growing up years, about Mummy and Papa and that though they were loving and gave me everything I wanted, there was always this nagging sense of being the second priority in their lives. And I especially missed having Mom at home when I came back from school to share my day. But despite this, I loved them both from the bottom of my heart and I knew that my love was reciprocated. Sometimes, I would feel a lavender fragrance floating in my room and a light touch on my forehead long after I had gone to sleep and I would know that it was Mom, who had come to my room to kiss me goodnight even though she was late and tired from work. While my mother's success, her brilliance and her reserve at times intimidated me and sometimes I even wished she was a more ordinary mother like my friends' mothers, I strove to be a super achiever like her and was driven by the fear that somehow, I would fail her.

I had always been more comfortable with Pa and he was the one who brought the element of fun in my life. Whenever he had time he played badminton with me and went swimming—both of which I loved. He taught me things, pampered me and called me his little princess. He also inspired my loved for math and science. He would take me to his office from a young age and would let me fiddle around with his computer. He would even take me to the factory and show me various machines and how they worked. This led to my love of all things technical and mechanical. I guess that my desire to be an engineer was because I looked up to him and wanted to emulate him.

In a twist of fate, however, things had turned upside down, and after the tragedy in my life somehow I had grown closer to Mom whereas there was a distance and aloofness in my relationship with Pa now.

I told Karuna (she insisted that I call her by her first name) about my school, my friends, my academic and sports achievements. Did I want to brag in front of her? Yes, maybe. Or perhaps I did not want her to judge me based on the recent event; maybe I didn't want her to think that I was a failure, a nobody, a promiscuous teenager. She encouraged me when I faltered and she did this gently, in a very non-invasive, non-threatening way. Only once in a while she prodded me on with one or two gentle questions especially when I got stuck telling her about Moh.

Once I finished, she said, 'I think that will be all for today Ananya. I will meet you again in a week's time.'

Was that it?! I don't know what I had expected from these sessions, but I'd hoped that they would do me some good. Maybe she could have sympathized with me or maybe she could have offered me some concrete advice. Instead, all she did was listen. I felt cheated! I'd bared things about myself which I had never shared with anyone before. And I had to go through these weekly sessions for two months. If I hadn't committed to Mom, I would have backed off that instant.

I felt very tired after the session and definitely didn't look forward to the next one.

All too soon, the time came. I was hoping that Karuna had forgotten the appointment or some emergency had come up so that she would not be able to make it, but no such luck.

I sat sulking in Pa's study reading a book and waiting for Karuna to come. She was irritatingly punctual. After a quick hello, I sat with my head tipped down. I was not going to do all the talking this time.

'Hey, you're looking nice, Ananya.'

'Thanks.'

'However, you need to put on a bit of weight. You're lucky you know, most people worry about losing weight, but you have the easy job of trying to put on weight,' she smiled. I noticed that she had a warm and pretty smile.

'Ananya, it is very important to take care of your body. Eat balanced meals. Have lots of fresh fruit juice. Get physically active. Find something that you will enjoy; a walk, tending the garden or playing a sport. Which sport did you say you liked— was it tennis?'

'No, badminton and swimming.' Really she should have paid more attention. I had told her this last time. 'Well, it is too cold to go swimming but once you have put on couple of kilos, you can certainly start playing badminton. By the way, which player do you like the most in badminton?'

'Amongst the Indian players I like Prakash Padukone's elegant game the most.' Then I rambled on as to what a shame it was that his daughter had chosen Bollywood over a career in badminton and then I finished by of course admiring my favourite Saina Nehwal, whom I liked the most amongst the current set of players. Karuna agreed wholeheartedly with my views on Deepika Padukone as well as Saina Nehwal and this improved my mood a bit. Just then she asked very quietly, 'You used to play badminton regularly with Moh too. Am I right?'

At the mention of Moh, I became quiet. Suddenly the sounds of the evening made themselves heard in the room. My thoughts went to the long warm evenings playing baddy with Moh. And then I thought of Rohit and everything that happened later. A tear rolled down my cheek.

As if sensing my thoughts, Karuna asked gently, 'Ananya, tell me about Rohit.'

Unlike last time, when I had talked hesitatingly and haltingly, this time the words gathered a momentum of their own and started flowing out rapidly, each word tumbling over the next. Maybe I wanted to purge myself of the deep, deep pain I was feeling. I told her everything—how I fell for him, his sophistication and his charm; how I was flattered by his interest in me especially over other girls; how I had imagined myself in love with him and how I'd even encouraged him. However, I'd trusted him completely and believed that he loved me too.

'So Ananya, how are you feeling now?'

What could I say? How could one begin to even describe the pit of misery and heartache that I had plummeted into? How can one even begin to talk about the pain of loss and shame that was so bad that it was almost physical, and which felt like a tight cast across my chest which hindered me from breathing?

I felt disgusted with myself for the pain and the shame I had inflicted on my parents. With my head bowed, I told her of my heartache, how it hurt terribly to think about Rohit and the way he had rejected me. I still couldn't believe that he had betrayed me.

It had to be some misunderstanding. I so wanted to meet

him once more and ask him why he did this to me. I had trusted him completely. How could I accept his betrayal? He knew my feelings for him too.

I told her of the humiliation that I had suffered in my school and that I never wanted to go back there.

I finished speaking and looked up. I saw compassion and sympathy in Karuna's eyes. However, she said little. 'On my way out, I will give your diet chart to your mother. Meanwhile take a lot of rest and I will see you again next week.'

Sharing the details of the events with someone who wouldn't carry the burden further and who wouldn't be judgemental helped me establish a comfort zone with Karuna. As I went back to my room, unlike last time, I was neither angry nor upset with her.

Suddenly I remembered that I had left the book I was reading in the study. As I went to pick it up, I heard muffled sobbing coming from inside the room.

I heard muffled voices. Mummy was sobbing and, in between her sobs, saying, '…but how could this even happen? Ananya has always been an example for others! We never saw this coming. She never even had a boyfriend; she had not even shown the slightest bit of interest in one. How could she change so much and that too without our even having any inkling about it? And her best friend's brother? She has known them since she was in preschool.'

I heard Karuna's soothing voice. 'Please calm down Mrs Sharma. Parents must understand that this is an age when teenagers are dealing with lots of issues. They have left their childhood behind, but are not adults yet. This creates a lot of confusion in their minds. Also, the hormonal changes that take place in their bodies add to their confusion. Attraction towards the opposite sex is a natural instinct, but we tend to overlook this fact as far as our kids are concerned. Compliments and attention from the opposite sex make them feel good. To top it, many a time, they face social and peer pressure as well.'

'Unfortunately, more often than not, this happens by someone highly trusted, like a brother's friend or a friend's brother and in some instances, even by family members such as a cousin or an uncle. The best defence against these incidents is knowledge. In most Indian homes, talking about sex is taboo. Many times parents procrastinate, thinking it is too early. But then it gets too late. If children are informed in time, they can cope better with the changes that are taking place inside them, become aware of the consequences and be watchful of the many lurking dangers.'

She continued, 'Also, maybe she didn't get the attention she was unconsciously craving for at home. She sought comfort outside—her friends, their parents and in Rohit.'

'What could we have done differently? And what should we do now, doctor?' Mom's voice was heavy with anguish.

'I have spoken to her at length. She is a very bright child and very loving too. She cares immensely about your opinion. She is feeling very guilty and is deeply traumatized right now. She will need all your help and support in the months and even years ahead to meet her full potential.' She paused for a minute and then said, 'You should encourage her to have open discussions with you. As parents you must make a conscious effort to spend quality time with her every day and take an active interest in her life. You have to help her find meaning in her life. Now I have to go. I wish all of you the very best. Please feel free to call or visit me anytime.'

24

In the evening, Sanjana and Nandini came to meet me and updated me on everything that was going on in school. While I felt a moment of regret at the thought of all the stuff I was missing out, I had no desire to go back to school.

'It's been a long time since we all went for a movie together. Let us go this weekend. What say?' Sanjana asked.

'Sounds like a great idea Sanjana. Let us go,' Nandini agreed.

'You both carry on, I will pass.' Though I loved movies, I had neither the will nor the stamina to go for one.

'Ananya, don't be such a spoil sport. Do come, at least this one time. You have to come.'

'Sanjana, don't insist. I'm not coming and with the board exams round the corner, I don't think you guys should be going too.'

'As if we care about grades,' they chorused and then Sanjana added, 'Well if you are not going, we are not going too.' I gave in to their collective emotional blackmail and they left smiling.

As it turned out, going for a movie wasn't a complete disaster. The good thing was that since most of the students were busy cramming for the board and competitive exams, we didn't meet anyone we knew. The good old combination of a time pass movie and popcorn, nachos and cold drinks was like balm for the soul.

At her suggestion, this time I was meeting Karuna in her clinic. On my way, I mused as to how our relationship had changed in the last one month or so. Initially sulking and sceptical about the meetings, I now looked forward to meeting her. In the last two sessions she'd made me talk about Rohit and helped me deal with my feelings regarding him in a way which made me feel more normal.

'It is natural to be attracted to someone of the opposite sex. However, you should also know your responsibilities and never put yourself in a position where you could be vulnerable. There is nothing wrong in making boys your friends, but it is better that you go out in groups. It is also advisable that you invite your friends over, especially guy friends, and introduce them to your parents. You should let your parents know where you are going and with who. This is for your own safety.'

She was warm, sympathetic, pragmatic and had a good sense of humour. What I liked the most about her was that she took genuine interest in knowing me. Somewhere along the way, rather than being just a doctor, she had become my friend, my confidante. I could have a very normal, day-to-day conversation with her, but somehow I benefited even from that, felt that just maybe some of the pieces of my life were falling back in place. Threads of conversations from the previous sessions ran through my mind.

'...I'm still so angry. I can't even describe how angry I'm with Rohit.'

Karuna said, 'I understand that Ananya. Okay tell me, what do you enjoy doing? When do you feel most energized?'

'I don't know… maybe while playing badminton.'

'Now listen Ananya. As regards Rohit, obviously he is not even worth the square foot he stands on and there is no point in you wasting time thinking about him. You can show your anger at him while hitting the shuttle cock as you play badminton, and this will rid you of your anger and relax you,' Karuna smiled as she said this.

'…Ananya, do you have any hobbies? Do you cook? Some people find cooking very relaxing.'

'Oh no! I can't cook to even save my life, Karuna. But I can whip up a mean bhelpuri, it's my speciality.'

'Okay, then why don't you make some for your mom and dad? I'm sure you will enjoy it and they will love it too. And don't forget to carry some for me. I absolutely love bhelpuri!'

Since Pa had been coming back a bit early at least a couple of times a week, he had persuaded me to start playing badminton again. And Karuna's advice had come in handy as every time I smashed the shuttlecock with more and more force.

Today Karuna was wearing a pastel, well-starched, cotton saree. She looked up from my chart, while munching on the bhelpuri I had carried for her and said with a smile, 'You were right Ananya, you do make the best bhelpuri.' She then added, 'I'm happy with your weight gain. Keep it up and soon you'll be as strong as a bull.'

'You got the wrong sex there Karuna, you should probably have said "cow".' I teased her and we shared a laugh.

Though I tried to relax with her, however, there were still

zillions of unresolved issues in my mind. My guilt, question marks about my future and my trauma meant that I continued to depend on sedatives for sleep. She must have sensed that something was amiss.

'Ananya, you have not told me everything. I can sense you are hiding something from me. Tell me, let everything come out.'

'How does she know?' I thought even as I wondered how to share what I felt about the guilt that I felt towards Mom-Dad as well as the baby. I started with the former, as it was easier to put in words.

In a very calm, but firm voice Karuna said, 'It's but natural that you feel bad about your actions and about upsetting your parents. You love them and don't want to hurt them. But please remember they are much stronger than you and can cope with this. You only need to think about yourself now and should lean on them for support. Nothing would heal them faster than to see your quick recovery and the smile back on your face.'

She said, 'Ananya, I understand that this has been a devastating experience for you. I can also imagine your guilt. But it's important for you to realize that you are not alone in dealing with the situation.' Slowly and soothingly, she told me how I must seek and accept support from my parents.

Then, I summoned all my strength to tell her what I would dare not acknowledge even to myself. It was so dark, so deep. My voice choking with unshed tears, I told her that what tore at my heart and flung me time and again into the depths of hell was my guilt about the loss of the baby. I felt as if by not wanting to have it, by hating being pregnant, I was responsible for the loss of her life. And my guilt overwhelmed me.

Karuna sat listening and then said very quietly, 'Ananya, it is natural that you feel this way. Making a connection with the baby will help you come to terms with your loss. You could get a plant in your child's memory and tend to it. Finally, the most important thing is that you must release your guilt. Dismiss the thought that your baby would be alive if you had done something differently, or if you hadn't for that fleeting second wished that you weren't pregnant. You may be searching for reasons and blaming yourself for the loss of your baby. Though tragic and harsh, it was probably nature's way of telling you that you were not ready for such a responsibility yet. Release yourself.'

'Find positive ways to get your feelings out—take up some hobby—write, paint, draw or cook. Don't worry if your work doesn't look or sound professional. No one else has to see it but you. Go back to your normal life and old friends as soon as possible.'

Just then a lady walked in carrying a tray with tea and biscuits.

As we sat sipping tea, her words kept echoing in my mind. Though she made sense, I was not sure I was strong enough to do any of the things she had advised me to. My void was infinite. The search for peace and consolation seemed fruitless. Though at the surface things were improving, deep inside my grief was so intense, that it was difficult for me to clear my mind enough to figure out what I could do to bring myself to face another day.

As if reading my mind, Karuna said that I should not think of running a mile to start with, but take a step at a time. I should be patient with myself. She said, 'Ananya, it's quite possible that you may not be functioning at the level you are used to. You may find it difficult to concentrate, or you might panic or feel frustrated. But time is the best healer. You will feel like yourself again eventually. We will meet again next week. I'm sure you will be feeling much better then.'

When I woke up the next day, I thought of following Karuna's advice. I went to the local nursery and looked around. I went to the rose section and saw a thick, very healthy plant with lovely huge fragrant pink roses. Next to it was a thin delicate rose plant with white roses. I immediately liked the smaller plant—flowers for the joy that I wished for the lost child and white for the purity of her soul.

As I paid for my tiny white plant, the maali told me that it was a rose creeper and I should make a rose trellis for it to climb on. I came back and planted it in a corner of the garden. As I looked at it, a deep sense of peace overtook me.

Just then my phone rang. It was Sanjana.

'Know what? I have just got my driver's license. Be ready and come out in ten minutes. Nandini is already here. I'm going to take you both for a spin. Mom's allowed it.'

Only the spin turned out to be bullock cart ride actually, because, for all her flamboyant attitude, Sanjana was a very careful driver. We were sitting in Vaishali enjoying its famed SPDP, when Sanjana said too casually, 'Anu, Amit has been asking about you. He's been meaning to call and also meet you, but was not sure about it. Why don't you give him a call or better still meet him for a coffee or something?'

'I don't know Sanjana. I like him, you know that. But I behaved really badly towards him when I was with Rohit. Even then he stood up for me in school and was very decent when I visited him during Diwali. However, I feel that I shouldn't take advantage of him,' I said, lowering my eyes.

'Stuff and nonsense! Amit's an old friend and besides he cares a lot about you. Why don't you just call him, what harm can it do?' Sanjana persisted.

'Let me see,' I said noncommittally though a bit pleased at the thought of reviving our friendship. It would mean so much to me.

Sanjana didn't leave it at that. When I reached home, Mom said, 'Anu, Sanjana told me that you are avoiding Amit. Why so? Why don't you go meet him or call him over? He's a nice, dear boy. Your father would be happy too.' She'd hardly finished saying this, when the phone rang, 'Anu, it's Amit.'

'Hey, Anu! How are you?'

'Doing okay. How is school?' I asked as a tight knot formed inside me thinking of my last day at school.

'Uh, fine I guess. Listen, on Friday after school we are all meeting at Coffee Express. Will you also join us?'

'We, as in?'

'Kabir, Dhruv, Dev and myself.'

I thought for a while. I, of course, knew all these guys and they were quite decent. Mom had already given her approval, so there wasn't any reason for me to not go.

'Can Sanjana and Nandini come too?'

'Of course, the more the merrier. See ya then.'

When I told Mom about the plan, she was quite happy. 'Yes, why not?' She added, 'I'll tell Papa to pick you up from there on his way back from work.' I happily nodded as I anyway didn't want to stay for long and it would give me an excuse to leave early. I was not to know then, but the meeting at the coffee shop would turn out to be life altering for me and maybe for Amit was well.

Amit was standing with his friends and looking very animated. Then as if sensing my eyes on him, he turned and his face grew sombre. Oh, is this is what I had become? A shadow that took everyone's laughter away?

And then he smiled again and with a nod in his friends' direction, started walking towards me. He smiled his impish smile. I always loved the way his eyes lit up when he smiled like this, eyes which were genuine and free of any guile.

'Hey Ananya, good to see you!'

I had been such good friends with Amit earlier, but now there was a certain awkwardness between us. Or maybe I was just imagining it. Kabir, Dev and Dhruv joined us and all lightly hugged me. I could feel warmth from them seeping into me. Just then I saw Sanjana and Nandini get down from an auto. Sanjana did a double take on seeing Dev with us; she'd always had such a crush on him. She quickly took out her mirror from her handbag, combed her hair and redid her lip gloss before walking towards us. Even in her worst avatar, she could have any guy eating out of her hands, but I guess some things never change, one of them being her desire to look perfect all the time, especially in front of good-looking guys.

I was really glad to see them both; it instantly made me feel more comfortable. We ordered dosas and coffees by the dozen. The guys were literally eating out of the waiters' hands. Things would disappear even before they touched our table. There was enough cackle and merriment at our table but I felt that something was missing. Something very important.

Though I had severed my friendship with Moh, I missed her more and more with each passing day and sometimes found myself picking up the phone to call her. However, I could never make that call.

The evening went off well. Everyone except me was in high spirits. Thankfully, they let me be most of the time. I saw Amit glance my way a couple of times with a look that I was not able to fathom. This was the first time we had all met socially and by the looks of it, it wasn't going to be the last either. As old bonds weakened, new ones were being forged, but they couldn't completely make up for the loss of the old ones.

25

I sat cross-legged, spine erect, at the centre of my bed.

I thought of the humungous change that my life had undergone. I couldn't connect to my earlier self—the over-ambitious, super achiever, self-centred Ananya with her well-known mood swings. I'd then never really appreciated the people around me—Pa and Mom, my friends and my teachers. I just took them for granted. And today, they had turned out to be my life lines.

I could not even connect with my earlier ambition of chasing the IITs. After all, wasn't it all just about me—Ananya wanting to top the class; Ananya cracking the IIT-JEE exams; Ananya chasing her dreams. All this held very little meaning for me now.

What is the meaning of life? What are we all here for? Is it all about I, me and myself? Is it all about the rat race in which everyone is running but no one is winning?

What is the learning for me in this, in the suffering that I have gone through? Do I continue to walk the same path that I was treading earlier? Or do I do something different, something that has a higher purpose in life?

What really is the big picture?

I have no idea how long I sat in this trance-like state; it could have been a few minutes or a few hours. However, when I got up, one thing was clear: I still hadn't found any answers.

'Karuna, I'm not sure what I want to do in the future. Earlier, I was just obsessed with being the class topper. I had very few friends. I don't know how to say this, but somehow now I feel that I led a very self-centred life.'

'I don't want to walk the same path anymore. I want to help others, people who are less privileged than I'm. I want to do something to give back to society. But I don't know what to do or how to go about it.'

'Ananya, that is a very nice thing to say. But what about your studies, your IIT dreams and plans for your career?'

'Karuna, I don't want to go back to my school. I can't stand the idea of meeting any old faces. The memory of what happened there will haunt me forever.'

'Ananya, take a small break from your studies, go back to your old friends and find time to do things that you enjoy. Your health and well-being should be the top priority right now. Drop a year and enrol in a different school next year.'

What Karuna said made sense. I had not studied in months and was in no shape to take any exams this year. I also could not bear the thought of going back to school and facing my classmates after what had happened.

She continued, 'Ananya, I support an NGO called Muskaan, which is committed to educating and empowering the girl child. These girls are from socially and economically disadvantaged communities, who traditionally have no access to schooling. The aim of the NGO is to break the cycle of illiteracy that girls from such communities are mired in. In many parts of the country, boys are still favoured while girls are left behind. Their illiteracy levels are shocking. Our experience shows that educating the girl child gives her confidence and not only transforms her but also her improved mental agility percolates into her home and her family. She becomes an agent for change. Later, in her turn, as a mother, she ensures the education of her children and objects to child marriages and other social ills. It creates a virtuous cycle benefiting society as a whole.'

She continued, 'You know Ananya, we are very fortunate that compared to other NGOs, we are relatively well funded. Though we don't have a surplus, we don't fall short either. However, we are always short of volunteers. You are a bright student, why don't you spend some time every week, as much as you can spare, teaching kids your favourite subjects, math and science?'

'And maybe, if you like teaching, you can even think of taking it up as a career once your education is complete. This will help you stay in touch with the subjects you love. And also utilize your talents and calibre for the benefit of many by passing on your love and passion for these subjects and shaping young minds.'

The idea held immense appeal for me. This is something I would so love doing. I had always loved teaching these subjects to Vidhi.

'Discuss this with your parents and let me know.'

'Anu, now drain the pasta in cold water,' Mom said as she taught me how to make my favourite penne pasta in pesto sauce.

'Mom, I wanted to discuss something with you,' I said.

Then I told her what Karuna had suggested. Mom was in complete agreement with her suggestions. But she was not sure if I was serious about not appearing for the IIT exams.

'Mom, for a long while, at least as long as I can remember the IIT entrance exams were a matter of life and death for me. I'm so over the whole thing now. Now I'm looking at the big picture and questioning what the purpose of our life really is. I'm very serious about doing social work along with my studies, but only with your permission.'

'Anu, whatever makes you happy makes us happy,' Mom said hugging me.

'Ananya, what are your happiest childhood memories?' asked Karuna.

In the previous session, I had filled out the volunteer form for the NGO Muskaan, and after that had visited the centre twice with Karuna. The whole experience of being the 'giver' rather than the 'taker' had been liberating for me. The girls, with their warm smiles, wide-eyed innocence and never-ending questions had captivated my heart, and dare I say, filled my void to an extent.

Karuna had been happy with my progress and she told my parents about this. Today was our eighth and last session.

At her question, I threw my mind back to my childhood and closed my eyes. I saw bright, colourful patches of light flashing behind my closed eyelids. I thought of the three of us having a gala time, numerous outings with Mom and Dad, our first foreign vacation together to Europe and the excitement surrounding it, topping the class, winning competitions and prizes. Like popcorn popping in a machine, various memories popped into my consciousness, but kept falling by the side.

I kept sitting. The colourful flashes of light behind my closed eyelids stilled and everything was a beautiful even black. Then a warm memory popped up which didn't fall by the side.

Memories of the many summer vacations spent with Nani, when I was both scolded harshly and pampered rotten, rose to my mind. And I knew then that nothing else stood a chance.

I answered Karuna's question, 'Summer vacations spent at Nani's place.'

'Then I suggest that you go and spend a month or so there and enjoy yourself. It would be a nice and interesting change for you.'

26

The familiarity and security of Nani's home, where I had spent so many of my childhood vacations, comforted my heart a little. She was a generous, warm and lively soul with a shock of white hair. She was also a down-to-earth, no-nonsense person and had a very practical, unsentimental way of dealing with things. She could be pretty strict also but her merry soft brown eyes crinkling at their corners would give her away more often than not. Nani was deeply religious—she knew the Gita, Ramayana, Sundar Kand, and numerous bhajans by heart—but not orthodox. She was extremely distraught when Nanaji passed away but didn't give up wearing bright colours or the red bindi as per the custom, as she believed that Nanaji wouldn't have liked her to live that way. They had been deeply in love and devoted to each other all their lives.

Nani and I had always gotten along like a house on fire.

Mom stayed with us for two days and then left. I don't know whether she told Nani anything or not. I think she did, but thankfully Nani didn't make any reference to it.

'I have told everybody that you are here during your prep leave.' I caught the subtle hint in her gentle, soft voice that it was what I was to say too in case someone asked.

I loved Bhilai with its clean tree-lined streets and decent, warm and well-educated people. The steel township combined the best of a large as well as a small city. It was cosmopolitan, modern and well-planned, and at the same time had a relaxed air about it. Being in a place where no one knew my story, relaxed and freed me in a way that I didn't think was possible.

'Anu Beta, today is Tuesday and on Tuesdays we have bhajans in the evening at our place. I have to go out for some shopping. Could you come along and help me?' Nani said, looking resplendent in a mango-yellow cotton saree with a red border.

'Of course Nani, give me a minute to freshen up.'

'It is good to have young blood around, I'm getting too old,' Nani murmured under her breath as she left the room. I smiled; everyone could age but her. She was spunky, all set to defy age and could put people half her age to shame. Still, it felt good to be useful.

'Nani, do you really believe in religion? Do you believe in God? Do you believe that chanting songs and mantras pleases God and makes our lives better?' I asked sitting cross-legged on the kitchen floor threading marigold flowers through a needle to make garlands for the evening. I was quite aware that this conversation would have been considered blasphemous in many households, but I was totally comfortable with Nani and I knew that she was secure enough in her beliefs and value system to tackle any questions.

Nani, sitting across me on the floor, continued kneading dough and I thought that maybe she hadn't heard my question. I was just about to repeat it when she spoke, 'No Beta, I don't believe in God, not in the way you mean it. I don't believe that rituals please God or enhance our karma. No, I do not believe in that at all.'

'But while I do not believe in God, I believe in goodness. And I believe traditions and rituals may not enhance our karma, but have a special place in our lives. They form a very important part of our social fabric and they connect people. They make for some wonderful and colourful memories, anchor societies and many a time, provide a much-needed means of escape—a much more holistic means of escape— than many other options. So my dear girl, do not underestimate their importance.'

'I know you youngsters don't give much importance to all these things, but sometimes following these traditions and rituals is all old people are left with,' her smile belied the seriousness of her words.

Nani was not highly educated, but she was a mine of wisdom. Counterintuitive it may be, but thinking of her and then myself, suddenly I had a feeling that education and wisdom were inversely related. Not a logical thought, but well, there it was!

The evening was a very colourful and noisy affair, and Nani was in her element—greeting guests, singing bhajans and at the end distributing prasad. I could see that she was very popular. To everyone who asked about me, she gave the same rehearsed answer. The fact that people met me and talked to me normally was a big relief and I found myself relaxing even more.

With the chant of the bhajans ringing in my head as I went to bed I thought about Nani. She was an awesome woman, a woman who lived life to the hilt and on her terms, a woman to derive inspiration from. She completed her education after getting married as she got married in her mid-teens and had Mom when she was about my age. Nani was a full-fledged mother at my age! The thought knocked the breath out of me.

I carried that thought to sleep.

I woke up with a start. But not kicking and screaming, only sobbing. It was exactly four months since the day I was rushed to the hospital.

The next day, just before going to bed, when Nani came to my room with my vitamins and sat down on my bed stroking my hair, I asked, 'Nani, sometimes I feel very lost and scared. All sorts of negative thoughts come and churn in my mind. I don't have any courage or strength left, I don't even feel whole or complete.'

'Anu Beta, only when gold is tempered in fire does it shine best.'

'I just want to be a simple girl, but even simple things seem to be getting impossible for me. I want to be like you—positive and at peace. How do I do that?'

Nani said, 'Anu, the mind is like a monster, either you tame it or keep feeding it, otherwise it will take hold of you. Try to tame your mind by engaging it in something spiritual such as reciting mantras or through meditation, and feed it by keeping it busy in wholesome activities like reading, playing or studying. This will make you strong.'

'The first step towards meditation is to concentrate on your breathing. Close your eyes and become aware of your breath—going in, then coming out. This will settle your mind and make you feel calm. Do it for about ten minutes, three or four times a day.'

Taking Nani's advice, I got up a little early the next day. In the beginning I found it very difficult to sit still and concentrate on my breath even for a few seconds. My mind kept delving into the past. But I willed myself to concentrate. Slowly, the seconds of successful concentration stretched into minutes and I managed to meditate for ten minutes at least thrice a day.

As I progressed with my meditation, I felt calmer.

Mom called every day and so did Sanjana and Nandini. Out of the blue, one day Amit also called me and hesitatingly asked how I was feeling.

Nani sure made me work for my stay—not that I minded. I got caught in the whirl of her energy—going for walks, buying provisions for the house, helping her with the cooking and tending to her garden—it was quite a job as she had a big garden. On top of all this we went visiting her friends where I would be treated like a malnourished kid with everyone insisting on feeding me. She even taught me a bit of embroidery—not the heavy stuff but a few simple stitches. I spent days embroidering handkerchiefs for her and Mom. My days were packed and I would fall into bed exhausted and go to sleep even before my head hit the pillow. My dependence on sedatives reduced and so did the frequency of my nightmares.

I don't know whether I was happy or sad to see Mom at the end of three weeks. I was strangely reluctant to go back, I knew going back meant facing my past. I had worn a simple pink-coloured salwar kameez, which Nani had bought me.

Mom was looking tired and haggard; it was a twenty-hour train journey and she had left straight from work. She had dark circles under her eyes and it looked as if she hadn't slept much.

Her face lit up when she saw me, 'Anu, you are looking very nice. And if I may say so, you have even put on a little weight which is suiting you so well!' Compliments from Mom were rare and it pleased me to get one.

I had tears in my eyes as I bid farewell to Nani. Mom had walked ahead to load the luggage in the waiting auto. 'I'm going to miss you Nani. How will I ever cope without you?'

'You will cope just fine. And you know what I think? I think that you will do very well indeed.'

'Now, run along. You will miss the train otherwise.'

'Love you Nani, bye,' I hugged her tightly before I ran to get into the waiting auto. I felt a certain heaviness descend on my heart as the auto turned the corner and headed towards the station.

27

All too soon we were back in Pune. Mummy put down a tray of food for me that had my favourite cream of mushroom soup, kofta curry, roti, peas pulao and curd. Giving me my vitamins, she said, 'Beta, now you must sleep. If you need anything, press this buzzer.' As she got up to leave, I caught her hand. I looked into her eyes and said, 'Mom, I'm sorry. So very sorry.' She sat down next to me and said very gently, 'Anu, it is not only your fault. I wish we had told you and warned you a bit about the ways of the world. So, if anything, we are equally at fault too. It is just that for us you were our little girl. We forgot that you had grown up.' It seemed Mom was fighting some inner battle of her own. 'You know we love you so much. Now you must not think about it at all and only look forward to the future. I will sit by you till you go to sleep.'

'So Anu, how was your stay at Nani's house?' Pa asked at breakfast. Instead of having my breakfast in my room, as I had been doing since my hospital stay, Mom had asked me to join them downstairs.

I looked at Pa, he was smiling at me. I felt as if after a long stormy night, probably the dawn was just breaking through. I couldn't see it yet, but I could sense it.

'Anu, I wanted to ask you something. There is a new township within Pune that has come up with excellent amenities and sports facilities, not far from here. While you were away, your Mom and I saw a few places there. They have nice bungalows there, like this one but bigger and we were thinking of maybe moving there. If you are okay with the idea, then you can go with Mom and finalize the place.'

Okay with the idea? I loved the idea. The thought of moving away from this dreadful neighbourhood where everyone treated us as if we had some kind of contagious disease breathed a new life into me. And to imagine that till sometime back, I had loved this place and the people here!

'Pa, I'm okay with it. Mom, let us go this weekend to see the houses.'

I loved the new bungalow and it had a huge lovely garden. This neighbourhood lacked the charm of the old place, but was new, swanky and modern. And the people here, a lot younger. The clubhouse had both a great indoors badminton court as well as a large swimming pool.

Sanjana and Nandini would occasionally join me for a swim and Pa would play badminton with me regularly on the weekends making up for my lost partner, Moh. I was able to manage my days well. But the nights were another matter altogether. After staying at Nani's and moving to the new place, my nightmares had reduced, but as and when they came, they would wrench my soul so much so that I was afraid of falling asleep.

That night, my nightmare revisited me as usual. I was running towards my child. But this time, after the nightmare had run its full course, towards its end the fog lifted suddenly and my child, dressed in white as against the usual black, walked towards me. I dropped down to my knees. The child, it was a girl, smiled and put her tiny arms around me pulling me into her embrace. What I felt is difficult to describe, but the closest I can say is that it was akin to a parched traveller, lost and wandering in a desert, suddenly finding water.

'I have some news to share,' Mom beamed over dinner. Neither Mom nor Dad were coming too late from work these days and almost everyday we all had dinner together. At first I resented this as I was used to having dinner alone and at a time of my choice, but slowly I had come to start looking forward to it as we all sat around the table and Mom-Dad shared the highlights of their day and asked me about mine.

'Spill the beans Sudha. I know you cannot keep a secret for long.' I was amused at Pa lightly teasing Mom.

'You know Kamal, I have been asking the seniors at my office to let me work from home. But they just kept sitting on my request. I got fed up with the wait and finally put in my papers last week. That somehow spurred them into action,' Mom beamed and added, 'And they have agreed! Now unless there is an important client visit or an internal meeting, most days I can work from home.'

'Hey Mom, that is really cool,' I jumped out of my seat to hug her.

Relieved of the burden of keeping long hours at work and the daily commute, Mom turned out to be amazing fun as I discovered to my astonishment. She was incredibly efficient at her work and joked, 'It is amazing, but when you don't have distractions around as is the case in office or a number of largely useless meetings to attend, you get all the work done in a fraction of time.' We did many things together—went shopping and combed the entirety of FC Road, MG Road and Koregaon Park, explored the city like tourists—visited Shinde Chhatri, Aga Khan Palace, Shaniwar Wada, Osho Ashram. Tried out new cafes and hotels. Went to various art exhibitions at Tilak Road, attended music concerts at Ganesh Krida Kendra and watched plays in Yashwantrao Chavan Auditorium.

I was discovering a new side to her. She was a very keen observer, intelligent, had a childlike curiosity and was kind hearted. I really started looking forward to these outings with her.

The next day Amit called and said, 'I have been thinking. I know you are very good at math, and it would help me a lot if you could come over for a couple of hours every day. I could discuss problems with you, it would be faster for me and I would be able to cover larger ground. You know the entrance exams are just round the corner.' My mouth fell open at his suggestion. I was in no shape to help anyone. I didn't know what to say or how to react. As the silence stretched on the phone he said softly and quietly, 'Hey, I'm sorry. Maybe it was a bad suggestion and I guess selfish of me as well. Ananya, I will understand if you are not comfortable doing this. I spoke without thinking.'

Oh no! He'd misinterpreted my silence. I would so love to help him. However, having dropped my IIT dream the way a snake sheds its old skin, I was so out of touch with things and studies—had not even looked at a math book in months—that I was not sure that I could help him out.

'No, Amit it is not like that. Of course, I would love to help you. It is just that I'm not sure if I can, I'm so out of touch.'

'Ananya, are you kidding? You are good, too good and you know that. There are many ways of solving a problem, and in Gollum's classes you were always the first to submit your papers. I think you have a knack of reaching the heart of the problem which gives you speed. It would be very useful for me to have that. In case you have the time and you are comfortable, it would be great if you could help me out.'

'Okay, but could you come over to my place for this?'

'Done.'

Often, Amit would call and come over in the evenings and after tackling math, we would go for a walk together. After his first visit, I had checked with Mom if it was okay if he came over and she had said it was. Amit too had curried her favour by spending some time chatting with her before coming up for his studies. She thought it showed his manners and reflected well on his upbringing. On most days, Amit was my only company, as everyone else got busy with interviews and entrance exams. Even Sanjana and Nandini were taking it seriously. It suited me fine. I preferred being by myself anyway, in my room reading a book. Sometimes I would sit in the garden for some time, facing my plant that I watered myself every day.

The other thing I did regularly was visit Muskaan. And to my amazement I discovered that probably the one thing I liked more than learning math and science was teaching these subjects. I would spend hours poring over the study material and trying to make it fun and interesting for the girls. The administration expressed their gratitude for my help, but I told them that it was I who was thankful to them and the children, as this was the only place where I managed to find a little peace.

And the tension of all the exams after reaching a pitch, finally started dying down as they started getting over. Now, only the wait for the results was left.

In the last couple of weeks, we—Amit, Dev, Kabir, Dhruv, Sanjana, Nandini and myself—formed a routine of meeting at some food joint or catching a movie together.

I think I was probably the last to notice. 'Where is Sanjana?' I asked, noticing her absence when we were sitting at the Pizza Hut in SGS mall. 'I see very less of her these days.' When I said this, everyone looked at each other and started laughing. I was puzzled. They wouldn't tell me but continued laughing as if I had told them the funniest joke or had suddenly sprouted horns. Finally, Nandini took pity on me and explained, 'Ananya, only you can be as blind as a bat. Now open your eyes and look around and see who else is missing.' I blinked and then focused—Amit, Dhruv, Kabir, Nandini and myself...we were all there...but wait a minute! Dev was missing too. Then everything clicked in place, they were always missing together—Dev and Sanjana. Nandini winked at me and said, '*Now* do you understand?'

And then they shared tales of their growing attraction for each other almost from the beginning of their friendship. They would sit next to each other in the movies, and even on picnics the two of them would walk off together, often laughing at some private joke that nobody else understood. The pieces of the puzzle started falling into place one by one. Yes, I too had seen this but had been too blind to register it.

Just then, as if my thinking about them had willed them to be here, Dev and Sanjana strolled in, hand in hand. They both looked so happy, their faces glowed and they seemed like the ultimate made-for-each other couple. I saw the joy in Sanjana's face and immediately identified with it—it was the same thing I had felt when I had aced the math Olympiad last year. Pure, unadulterated joy. I couldn't help crossing my fingers behind my back to ward off bad luck from them. Seeing them together, so happy and in love, banished some of the darkness from my soul.

Over the next couple of weeks, we were quite amused to watch their romance blossom further. They were inseparable. Of course they joined us for many outings, but even then they would be lost in a secret world of their own. Their love for each other, the uncomplicated and carefree life of my friends and everyone's tacit support for me, is what, I believe, sustained me during the blackest days of my life. I was thankful to God for giving me each of them—Amit, for his unaffected simple manner and a big, generous and kind heart; Nandini and Sanjana for their unstinting support, understanding and the element of fun; Dev, loving and great looking and taking care of Sanjana; Dhruv and Kabir, one the foodie and the other the prankster, who added immense colour to our lives. Overall, I couldn't have asked for a better set of friends.

I was getting stronger every day. With Mom and Pa's care, help from my friends and by following Nani's and Karuna's advice, my life had now almost settled into a routine. I was meditating regularly now and felt calmer.

The next day, I went downstairs to see my rose plant. Oh! My tiny plant looked so very pretty; overnight, it had sprouted tiny new leaves and was that... was it really... could it possibly be?

I bent closer to get a better look and yes, sure enough!

There was a small bud peeping shyly from between the leaves, so unsure of its place in this new world. My heart soared and I sat down in front of the plant for a long while, unmindful of the mud getting on my jeans.

28

With all the entrance exams getting over, we decided to maximize our time together as very soon, we would be splitting up. Long drives, swimming and hanging out at coffee shops took up most of our time. As for Ma and Papa, they were happy to see me relaxed after such a long time. How one month flew by, I have no idea, and all too soon, it was time for the results to be declared.

Various college results came pouring in one after the other. Sanjana got admission for B. Com in NMIMS College, Mumbai; Nandini got into the JJ School of Arts in the same city; Amit, Dev, Dhruv and Kabir secured admission in the Pune College of Engineering. Kabir and Dhruv were ecstatic with the news; this is what they had wanted. Amit and Dev were delighted too, but they waited for their IIT results to be declared.

And then the unthinkable happened. While Dev got through IIT JEE, Amit didn't. Everyone was so sure that Amit would make it. It was just not possible. Dev was confident that he will get the branch of his choice at IIT Bombay and to be in the same city as Sanjana was a double whammy for him. To my surprise, Amit took the rejection rather well. He wasn't devastated or anything as I would have expected him to be. Instead, he seemed put down but just for a while and was his usual cheerful self soon enough. The guy was truly amazing. My respect for him went up many notches.

I had continued spending as much time as possible at Muskaan on Sundays where Amit would mostly join me. I looked forward to going there all week, loved the time spent there and would leave with great reluctance.

However, I couldn't shake Moh's memories away. Always, at her memory, I felt a dull ache in my heart. She would have appeared for her medical entrance exams. There was this thought at the back of my mind—maybe it was that spider-like thread, almost invisible, but strong, that connected soul buddies—that she too missed me.

Today, Sanjana was coming for a sleepover, something I was looking forward to. We quickly wrapped up dinner and went up to my room.

After a chatathon, my eyes were fluttering close and I snuggled in deeper in my quilt. I reached to switch off my bedside lamp when Sanjana said, 'Anu, you know what? The thought of stepping out of home and going to college has made me feel so grown up. Sometimes I really laugh to myself when I remember the old times—it all seems so childish now.' She looked beautiful in her floral printed, spaghetti-strap night gown with the soft yellow light reflecting off her shoulders.

'Remember Amit throwing a plastic lizard at you in class XI, that saw you both getting detention. Then there was that day when our math teacher, Shastri sir had caught us all passing notes in the class and sent us out of the room. The same day there was also the sleepover at Moh's place, and you were still sulking about it.'

Yes, of course I remembered.

The memory lane is most slippery and treacherous. You just stand on its edge and, before you know it, you are slipping down fast and unable to navigate in a structured way. After all, so much had happened in my life. And yes, I now remembered that day clearly. Feeling traumatised at a punishment from a teacher! It was almost laughable now. And I remembered the night at Moh's place when Sanjana had teased me about Amit; the night when I fell for Rohit. That sleepover had totally changed my life. Our worries, our fights, our issues—all that seemed so insignificant now specially after what I had been through.

I consciously stemmed the flow of thoughts as I sensed the direction they were taking.

Aloud I said, 'Yes I remember everything. But Sanjana now I want to firmly look forward and not dwell in the past. Also I'm very happy that everyone in our group has got what they wanted. Except Amit. Somehow, I can't help but feel bad about him. I know he looks happy enough to be here in Pune, but really he deserved better. I still can't understand how he didn't get through IIT JEE.'

'But he did, it was only because…,' Sanjana didn't finish and clamped a hand over her mouth even as her eyes grew wide with horror.

'Sanjana, what were you saying? He got through? What are you talking about?'

'Anu, I'm really sorry. But I can't say anything more. I promised.' She sat with her head down, looking as dejected as a wet pup, and guilty.

'Sanjana, for heaven's sake just shut up and be sensible for once! What is this? Why did he not take up his IIT admission?'

I was losing it. I didn't know what it was, perhaps the look on my face, but finally Sanjana relented and said, 'Amit made us all swear to secrecy, but the fact is that he did get through. But since he wanted to be near you and be there for you, he chose to give it up. He said he was anyway getting his branch of choice in Pune, so it really was fine.'

I felt as if someone had dunked me with a bucket of icy cold water. Could this be true? I suddenly remembered how surprised I was at Amit not getting through IIT and how well he had bounced back from the 'setback'.

'You are insane. I don't believe you,' I whispered, not wanting it to be true. How could I ever live with something as humungous as this?

'Hey, why don't you check the website? The results came out just a week back. Maybe they have not taken them off yet.'

My bedside lamp provided the only illumination in the room. I went to my table and with trembling hands switched on the laptop. Sanjana stood behind me, her hands resting on the back of my chair. I typed in 'Amit Nagarajan' and hit 'Go' and in a flash of a second the result appeared, 'Selected. Rank 220'.

My hand flew to my mouth and I felt sick. Not only did he get through but rank 220 was phenomenal. I got up from the table and blindly walked towards the bed. Sanjana stopped me and hugged me, 'I think he really cares for you Ananya. He was heartbroken with what happened to you.'

'He has really gone too far. What does he think of himself? I will meet him tomorrow and give him a piece of my mind.'

'Anu, chill. Be gentle with him. You were not the only one who was hurt; others may have suffered too,' Sanjana said in a soft voice.

29

I was like avenging fury personified. Since the Diwali visit last year, I had not been to Amit's house, only he had been coming over. Maybe it was my overwrought nerves, but last Diwali when we had visited them I had sensed a slight coldness, hardly discernible, in Aunty's attitude. She was too well mannered, too gracious a host to have made any obvious gesture. Moreover, one could hardly blame her for that. Despite being regular visitors before, Uncle and Aunty had not come to our house to wish us on Diwali for the last two years. I'm not sure if Mom and Pa noticed this, but I surely did. Normally I won't have gone to Amit's house, but the occasion demanded that normalcy be set aside and some serious measures be undertaken.

I rang the bell—once…twice…thrice… I could hear the echo of the bell chiming inside the house. I knew Aunty would be away at her school, but where was Amit? Irritated, I rang the bell again, and then again.

'Hang on…coming!'

'Ananya…what's up? Everything okay?' Amit stopped dead in the act of drying his hair. The wet towel hung limply on his shoulders as he caught me by my shoulders and shook me, lines of worries etched on his face.

'No, nothing is okay! Who do you think you are, some macho superhero?' I shouted at him.

'Will you at least tell me what happened?' Amit said in a firm and patient voice as if talking to a child. Had he gotten angry too, I would have probably backed off. But his even tone goaded me even more. I shrugged off his hands from my shoulders and said, 'No, nothing has happened! No one has given up the biggest dream of his life, his IIT seat for my sake. No, of course nothing has happened. What *has* happened?'

As Amit stood still, probably trying to absorb the scene unfolding in front of him, a self-righteous murderous rage rose inside me and I started showering fists on him, 'And you call yourself a friend. You are a liar, a cheat!'

Amit stood like a steady rock taking my blows and then silently, quietly caught hold of both my hands and pinned them to my side. 'Yes, I lied to you, but only because I care for you and am very fond of you. I wanted to be around you. And getting into IIT is just a desirable thing for me, not my dream. Something else is.' His tone had changed but I barely registered it.

'Amit, I really don't know what to say. You have done something so humungous, I will forever be in your debt. How will I ever repay you for your kindness?' my fury spent, I was sobbing now.

'It is a friendship we have Ananya, and a very special one too. It is not buying goods from a bania that you are talking about repaying!'

'Look at me,' he said. I raised my head. Through the mist in my eyes, I saw his ruffled raven-black wet hair with water drops hanging from some strands, a cut on his left cheek probably from shaving and intense, very intense midnight black eyes. Eyes in which the usual laughter and mischief were absent now.

'I love you Ananya. And I only want one thing from you. I want to see you happy. I want that smile to be back on your lips.' I suddenly realized that in the act of pinning down my hands, we were standing quite close to each other, very close in fact. Even as his words rang true, I felt flustered.

His eyes twinkled, but he seemed a little nervous too. Then as if shaking off the tension, he said, 'They say opposites attract and see how true that is. I'm smart you are loony, I'm fast you are slow, I'm the prince you are the frog.' I knew where this was going, so freeing my hands from his grip I moved to whack him, but he ran away. I chased him around the hall as he repeated it was true. 'If you were not loony and slow, you would have worked this out for yourself a long time back!' he shouted over his shoulder, dodging me. Then he stopped and caught hold of my wrists. His raven black eyes were on me again.

He leaned closer and then kissed me softly on my forehead. 'Ananya, I meant every word I said. I love you.'

Even as the softness of his words started sinking in, I chided myself that there was work to be done first. I would dwell on what he'd said and my own feelings later. I couldn't let him distract me from the purpose of my visit by his sweet talk. I pulled myself back, cleared my throat and said sweetly, very sweetly in fact.

'You love me, Amit?'

Amit nodded and smiled sheepishly.

'You want to see me happy, Amit?' I said.

'Yes. More than anything else.'

I continued, a bit more seriously now, 'Well, Amit, what has happened can not be undone, how much ever I wish it. However, if you really want to see me happy then promise you *will* join IIT. I would never be comfortable with myself if you don't. Fortunately, it is not too late.'

'Are you sure about this, Ananya? I really don't want to be away from you.'

'Amit, I know you were keen on IIT Bombay. How far is that really from Pune—just a three-hour drive. Come on Amit, we can Skype daily and we will meet during long weekends and your semester breaks.'

'And, Amit, I'm much better now, really.'

He came forward and embraced me in a bear hug and I felt a thousand suns warming my insides.

'Anu, everything will be okay. I love you and am very proud of you.'

I went to the washroom to freshen up and saw that my tears had made dust streaks across my cheeks. I looked frightful but that was nothing new.

30

I was waiting for Amit at Coffee Express. He was in Pune during his first semester break. I looked at the watch and frowned. Amit was late, this was quite unusual. I was just fumbling in my handbag, trying to find my mobile when I felt someone slide into the opposite seat. I tried to make my face severe, to tick off Amit for being late, but I froze when I saw that it was not Amit, but Moh.

I had thought so much about her in the last one year, but when I saw her, I didn't know how to react. As our eyes met, I felt a surge of emotion through me. Here was my best buddy. Since kindergarten, we had shared everything with each other—our secrets, happiness and pain. And that one foolish afternoon had spoilt everything between us. However, surprisingly, I was now able to cope with my pain and, as I looked at her, I knew that she too had moved on and learnt to deal with it.

I ordered coffees for both of us and asked how she was doing. Moh told me that she had got admission in the AFMC College in Pune and was now pursuing her MBBS there.

Then, as if she couldn't bother to put up with the small talk, she said, 'Things have been very tough at our place too.

Though Mom and Pa had kind of protected Rohit at your place, they were both extremely unhappy and upset at what happened with you and also with the way Rohit had behaved. To cut a long story short, Rohit completed his studies by taking up a night job as Pa cut off his allowance. After that, he got a decent job with an IT company. I know this because he kept e-mailing me, though I never replied. He did very well in the first year of his job. However, as the economy was hit by recession his company downsized and he got the pink slip. Not only that, he got into drugs. Rohit is now in rehab, Mom left for the US a week ago and will stay with him for a couple of months, while he recovers. And Anu, he has asked me to pass on his apologies to you. I think he always did regret what happened, but it is only now that he has got the courage to admit it.'

Moh and I sipped our coffee, each lost in her own web of misery, thoughts of the childhood lost and a friendship broken.

The news about Rohit's downfall should have made me happy. He who had turned my life into a living nightmare was now himself in need of help. But I didn't feel elated, maybe because I had managed to find meaning in my life now. I closed my eyes and prayed that he would emerge a stronger and better person after the sordid experience and maybe his apologies were already a step in that direction.

Moh then asked me about what I was doing and my future plans. I told her everything—about my sessions with Karuna, her help in my finding a purpose in my life. I told her how I had joined another school to complete Class XII. Though the school was halfway across the city, no one there knew my history and I was able to concentrate on my studies.

I told her about my work at Muskaan and how it had

liberated me and how I now planned to be a teacher once I completed my studies.

Even our second cup of coffee was now over. We both got up and Moh hugged me and left. I don't know what course our friendship would take in the future, but at least for now I felt at peace.

As I picked up my bag and turned to leave, I saw Amit standing near the entrance of the coffee shop. So he'd set this up. He knew me so well. I smiled at him and we left together.

It was a lovely Sunday morning. Winter had just set in. I went downstairs to water my plant, which had spread itself beautifully over the trellis and was laden with beautiful fragrant white roses.

Today I decided to slightly stretch my usual five-minute shower. I massaged my hair with warm coconut oil, got Amma to make me her special face pack with besan, turmeric, malai, dried and crushed orange peel and honey that always worked wonders for me. By now, my face pack had dried and I stepped in for a leisurely shower.

As I rinsed off the shampoo from my long hair, images from the past year flashed in front of my eyes. I could still feel a twinge of sadness for the life that was not to be, though she would always hold a special place in my heart. I silently said a prayer for her soul. I remembered the dark months that followed when even taking a single breath seemed to take a huge effort.

I stepped out of the shower and dried myself, my train of thought continuing.

I envied my earlier carefree and innocent self, naïve, starry eyed and gullible. What a far cry from who I had become now. The physical and the mental scars may fade with time, but they couldn't take me back to being the child I was. My smile took longer to reach my eyes…my eyes that had seen too much of human nature…and my heart that would always take longer to trust someone. I would gladly trade the acquired wisdom and experience to go back in time. If I could, I would do things differently.

But life had given me a second chance and with help from my dear friends, especially Amit, I was able to meet the challenges. As I finished drying myself, I examined myself critically in the full-length mirror. I had put on a bit of weight and didn't look like a scarecrow anymore. My earlier bra-length hair, in the absence of any attention from the hairdressers in the past one year had grown till my waist and, post the oil massage, shampoo and conditioning, was shining glossily.

I thought I would give my favourite jeans-T-shirt combination a skip for once. I slipped on a lemon green Lucknowi chikan kurta and churidar. I wore the silver jhumkis Mom had given me. I highlighted my eyes with a thick application of kohl and pushed my spectacles up my nose. I dried my hair and made one long plait loosely done and swung it over my shoulder. Finally, I applied lip gloss and was all set to leave.

Just then my phone rang. As I saw 'Amit calling' I smiled to myself. He was punctual as always. It was time for him to pick me up and go to Muskaan. I took the call and said, 'Will be down in five minutes.'

I had finally laid all my ghosts to rest. I walked down the stairs with a spring in my step.

Out came the sun and dried up all the rain,
And the incy wincy spider climbed up the spout again!

Acknowledgements

The journey into the world of fiction has been long but interesting, with plenty of twists and turns along the way.

I couldn't have made this journey but for the people in my life. Sriram, this book would not have been possible without you. Your invaluable inputs and feedback on the various drafts—and there were many—made this book what it is. Your support and motivation also kept me going, especially during those times when I was on the verge of giving up.

To my family, which supports me in all my ventures and from whom I draw strength. Appa, I am blessed to have you with us and there is so much I learn every day from your simplicity and positive outlook. Mom, I am whatever I am because of you. I am really lucky to have the most loving, cool and hip mother. Sriram, my soulmate, thanks for teaching me to fly. My sons, Aditya and Ritwik, who add colour to my life. There is not a dull moment with you two around. Your unaffected behaviour, unconditional love and brand new way of looking at things are like a breath of fresh air. My dear brother, Ashish, who has always been there for me, in good times and bad, and who has always motivated me to reach higher. My sister-in-law, Ruchi, in whose company I have

Shilpa Gupta

always found comfort and joy. Athimbeyer, Meena and Viji, for being there.

Simmu, a dear friend and ex-colleague, painstakingly edited the first drafts of my book. I know how much effort and time you put into it without even knowing what the outcome would be. I was really touched and owe you one.

Kaniskha, CEO and founder Writer's side, a big thank you to you for helping my manuscript make the transition to a book. I really counted on your advice and feedback, especially since *Ananya* is my debut novel.

Ahmed, for reposing faith in Ananya's story and being a friend on this journey.

My publishers, Rupa Publications India, for making my dream come true.

Lipi, it was a pleasure working with you. I really respect your work ethics and adherence to timelines. Prerna, thanks for seeing my book through the last milestone.

Charu and Niru, for your invaluable inputs and suggestions.

And, finally, to all my friends in Pune and Mumbai, who are not only great fun to be with but also my lifeline. You know what you mean to me.